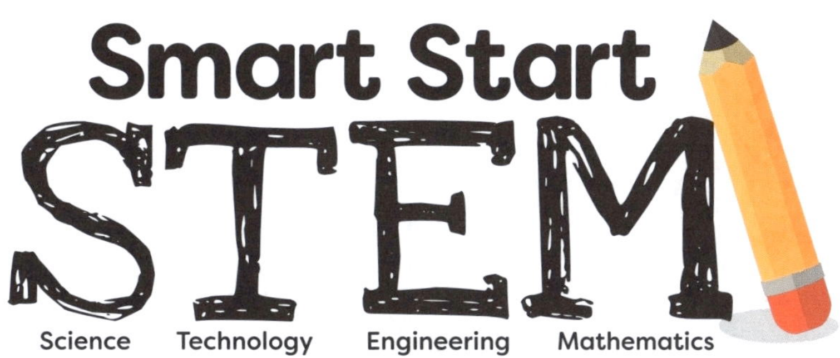

Writing: Tiffany Rivera
Barbara Allman
Content Editing: Lisa Vitarisi Mathews
Copy Editing: Laurie Westrich
Art Direction: Yuki Meyer
Cover Design: Yuki Meyer
Illustration: Ann Iosa
Design/Production: Yuki Meyer
Jessica Onken

EMC 9926

Visit
teaching-standards.com
to view a correlation
of this book.
This is a free service.

Correlated to Current Standards

Congratulations on your purchase of some of the finest teaching materials in the world.

EVAN-MOOR CORP.
phone 1-800-777-4362, fax 1-800-777-4332.

18 Lower Ragsdale Drive, Monterey, CA 93940-5746. Printed in China.

006

CPSIA: Asia Pacific Offset Ltd, Kowloon, Hong Kong [4/2021]

Contents

Life Science

Earth Science

General Materials List

- aluminum foil
- apple
- blueberries (10)
- cardboard
- clay or putty
- cotton balls
- digital camera (optional)
- glue
- gumdrops
- magnet
- marshmallows (mini and regular)
- metal objects: paper clip, pin, screw, bolt, etc.
- paint
- paper
- paper plate
- paper towel rolls
- pennies (22)
- plastic cups (25)
- playdough

- popsicle sticks
- rocks
- rubber bands
- sand or sandpaper
- scissors
- shoe box
- stapler
- straws
- string
- stuffed animal, baby doll, or other toy
- styrofoam cups (5)
- tape
- timer or stopwatch
- tissue boxes
- toothpicks
- tub or bucket
- water
- wax paper
- wood skewers

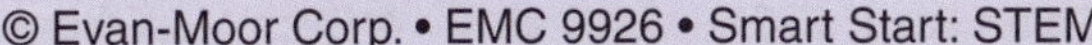

How to Use This Book

STEM: Science, Technology, Engineering, and Math

The STEM activities and challenges in this book are designed to be fun! Children are invited to think creatively and explore different ideas to solve problems. They engage in questioning, problem solving, collaboration, and hands-on projects. Parents act as facilitators, guiding their children through the problem-solving process and providing encouragement. The lessons in this book will help children understand science concepts and provide a foundation for completing the STEM challenges. Children who have opportunities to do STEM challenges learn to think critically and develop skills to become problem solvers who can find solutions to real-world problems.

Science Texts and Stories

Read the science text and the science story to your child. Discuss how the illustrations or photos help your child better understand the science concept. Help your child make connections between the science concept in the story and his or her own life.

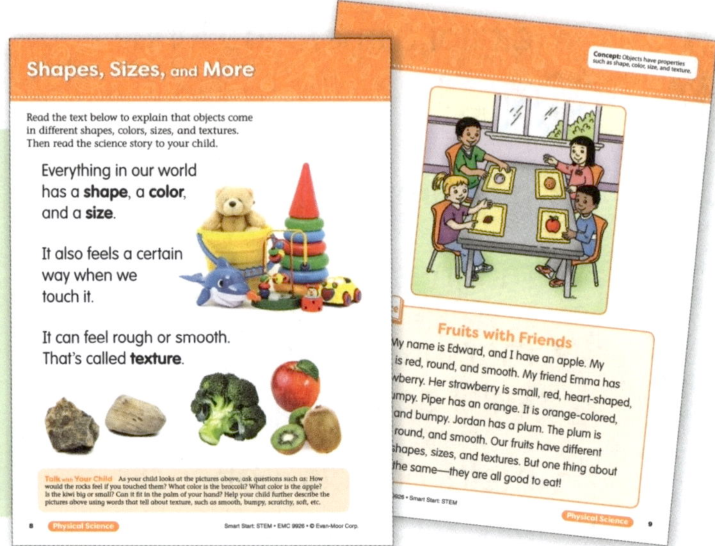
Shapes, Sizes, and More

Read the text below to explain that objects come in different shapes, colors, sizes, and textures. Then read the science story to your child.

Everything in our world has a **shape**, a **color**, and a **size**.

It also feels a certain way when we touch it.

It can feel rough or smooth. That's called **texture**.

Talk with Your Child As your child looks at the pictures above, ask questions such as: How would the rocks feel if you touched them? What color is the broccoli? What color is the apple? Is the kiwi big or small? Can it fit in the palm of your hand? Help your child further describe the pictures above using words that tell about texture, such as smooth, bumpy, scratchy, soft, etc.

8 Physical Science Smart Start: STEM • EMC 9926 • © Evan-Moor Corp.

Concept: Objects have properties such as shape, color, size, and texture.

Fruits with Friends

My name is Edward, and I have an apple. My … is red, round, and smooth. My friend Emma has …wberry. Her strawberry is small, red, heart-shaped, …mpy. Piper has an orange. It is orange-colored, … and bumpy. Jordan has a plum. The plum is … round, and smooth. Our fruits have different shapes, sizes, and textures. But one thing about the same—they are all good to eat!

…926 • Smart Start: STEM Physical Science 9

Activities

The written activities practice science concepts as well as basic skills such as writing, matching, and sequencing. Provide your child with support by reading the directions and answering any questions he or she may have.

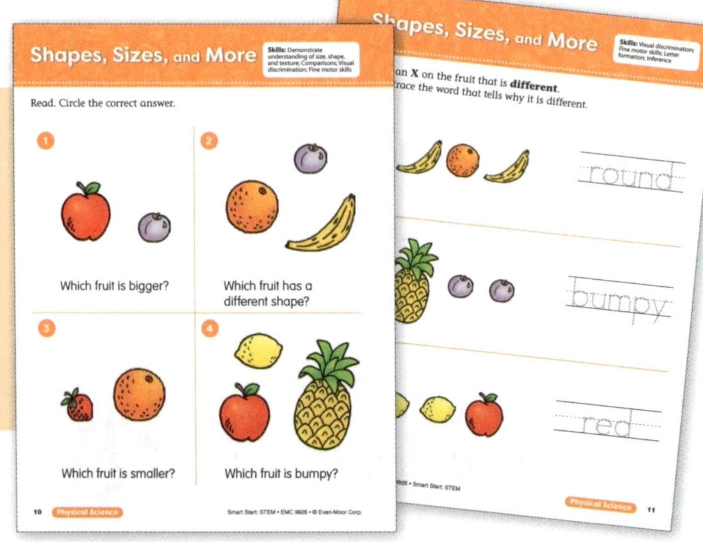
Shapes, Sizes, and More

Skills: Demonstrate understanding of size, shape, and texture; Comparisons; Visual discrimination; Fine motor skills

Read. Circle the correct answer.

1 Which fruit is bigger?

2 Which fruit has a different shape?

3 Which fruit is smaller?

4 Which fruit is bumpy?

10 Physical Science Smart Start: STEM • EMC 9926 • © Evan-Moor Corp.

Shapes, Sizes, and More

Skills: Visual discrimination; Fine motor skills; Letter formation; Inference

…an **X** on the fruit that is **different**.
…race the word that tells why it is different.

round

bumpy

red

…926 • Smart Start: STEM Physical Science 11

STEM Stories

Read the STEM story to your child. Discuss the illustration and the problem in the story. Ask your child to share his or her ideas about how to solve the problem.

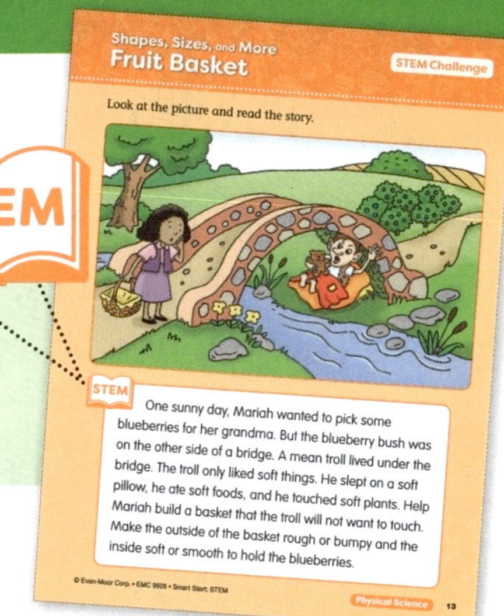
Shapes, Sizes, and More
Fruit Basket
STEM Challenge

Look at the picture and read the story.

STEM

One sunny day, Mariah wanted to pick some blueberries for her grandma. But the blueberry bush was on the other side of a bridge. A mean troll lived under the bridge. The troll only liked soft things. He slept on a soft pillow, he ate soft foods, and he touched soft plants. Help Mariah build a basket that the troll will not want to touch. Make the outside of the basket rough or bumpy and the inside soft or smooth to hold the blueberries.

© Evan-Moor Corp. • EMC 9926 • Smart Start: STEM
Physical Science 13

STEM Challenges

Use the information in the STEM Challenge to help you facilitate your child's experience.

- Read the Objective, the Challenge, and the Suggested Materials list. Then set up a place for your child to work. Feel free to add any materials you feel are appropriate for the challenge.
- Explain the Objective and the Challenge to your child. Then guide your child through the steps of the STEM Process. It is important to note that there is not a "right" answer to a STEM Challenge. Children should be encouraged to explore their ideas and their creativity.

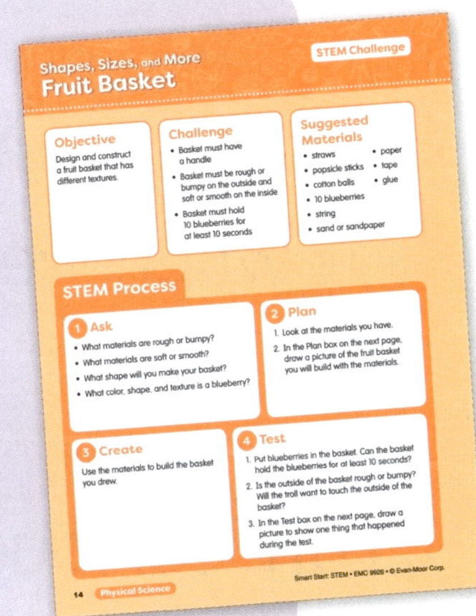
Shapes, Sizes, and More
Fruit Basket
STEM Challenge

Objective
Design and construct a fruit basket that has different textures.

Challenge
- Basket must have a handle
- Basket must be rough or bumpy on the outside and soft or smooth on the inside
- Basket must hold 10 blueberries for at least 10 seconds

Suggested Materials
- straws
- popsicle sticks
- cotton balls
- 10 blueberries
- string
- sand or sandpaper
- paper
- tape
- glue

STEM Process

1 Ask
- What materials are rough or bumpy?
- What materials are soft or smooth?
- What shape will you make your basket?
- What color, shape, and texture is a blueberry?

2 Plan
1. Look at the materials you have.
2. In the Plan box on the next page, draw a picture of the fruit basket you will build with the materials.

3 Create
Use the materials to build the basket you drew.

4 Test
1. Put blueberries in the basket. Can the basket hold the blueberries for at least 10 seconds?
2. Is the outside of the basket rough or bumpy? Will the troll want to touch the outside of the basket?
3. In the Test box on the next page, draw a picture to show one thing that happened during the test.

14 Physical Science
Smart Start: STEM • EMC 9926 • © Evan-Moor Corp.

STEM Journals

The STEM Journal is based on the engineering design process. Provide support by reading the labels and any other text to your child. Explain to your child in simple terms that planning, creating, testing, and recording are all part of completing a STEM Challenge.

Shapes, Sizes, and More
Fruit Basket
STEM Journal

Plan

Create: Use materials to build your project.

Test

Did it work? ☐ yes ☐ no

© Evan-Moor Corp. • EMC 9926 • Smart Start: STEM
Physical Science 15

Shapes, Sizes, and More

Read the text below to explain that objects come in different shapes, colors, sizes, and textures. Then read the science story to your child.

Everything in our world has a **shape**, a **color**, and a **size**.

It also feels a certain way when we touch it.

It can feel rough or smooth. That's called **texture**.

Talk with Your Child As your child looks at the pictures above, ask questions such as: How would the rocks feel if you touched them? What color is the broccoli? What color is the apple? Is the kiwi big or small? Can it fit in the palm of your hand? Help your child further describe the pictures above using words that tell about texture, such as smooth, bumpy, scratchy, soft, etc.

Concept: Objects have properties such as shape, color, size, and texture.

Fruits with Friends

My name is Edward, and I have an apple. My apple is red, round, and smooth. My friend Emma has a strawberry. Her strawberry is small, red, heart-shaped, and bumpy. Piper has an orange. It is orange-colored, round, and bumpy. Jordan has a plum. The plum is purple, round, and smooth. Our fruits have different colors, shapes, sizes, and textures. But one thing about them is the same—they are all good to eat!

Shapes, Sizes, and More

Skills: Demonstrate understanding of size, shape, and texture; Comparisons; Visual discrimination; Fine motor skills

Read. Circle the correct answer.

1

Which fruit is bigger?

2

Which fruit has a different shape?

3

Which fruit is smaller?

4

Which fruit is bumpy?

Shapes, Sizes, and More

Skills: Visual discrimination; Fine motor skills; Letter formation; Inference

Draw an **X** on the fruit that is **different**.
Then trace the word that tells why it is different.

1 

2 

3  

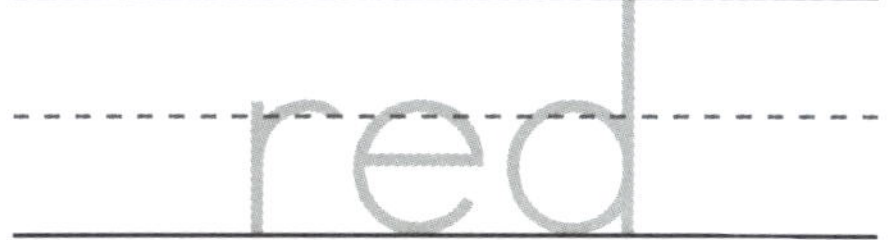

Shapes, Sizes, and More

Skills: Recognize shapes; Matching; Visual discrimination; Fine motor skills

Draw a line to match the shape with a food item.

square

circle

triangle

Fruit Basket

Look at the picture and read the story.

STEM

One sunny day, Mariah wanted to pick some blueberries for her grandma. But the blueberry bush was on the other side of a bridge. A mean troll lived under the bridge. The troll only liked soft things. He slept on a soft pillow, he ate soft foods, and he touched soft plants. Help Mariah build a basket that the troll will not want to touch. Make the outside of the basket rough or bumpy and the inside soft or smooth to hold the blueberries.

Fruit Basket

STEM Challenge

Objective

Design and construct a fruit basket that has different textures.

Challenge

- Basket must have a handle
- Basket must be rough or bumpy on the outside and soft or smooth on the inside
- Basket must hold 10 blueberries for at least 10 seconds

Suggested Materials

- straws
- popsicle sticks
- cotton balls
- 10 blueberries
- string
- sand or sandpaper
- paper
- tape
- glue

STEM Process

1 Ask

- What materials are rough or bumpy?
- What materials are soft or smooth?
- What shape will you make your basket?
- What color, shape, and texture is a blueberry?

2 Plan

1. Look at the materials you have.
2. In the Plan box on the next page, draw a picture of the fruit basket you will build with the materials.

3 Create

Use the materials to build the basket you drew.

4 Test

1. Put blueberries in the basket. Can the basket hold the blueberries for at least 10 seconds?
2. Is the outside of the basket rough or bumpy? Will the troll want to touch the outside of the basket?
3. In the Test box on the next page, draw a picture to show one thing that happened during the test.

Shapes, Sizes, and More

Fruit Basket

STEM Journal

Plan

Create: Use materials to build your project.

Test

Did it work? ☐ yes ☐ no

Solids and Liquids

Read the text below to explain that water can change from a liquid to a solid and back again. Then read the science story to your child.

Water is a **liquid**. A liquid flows from one place to another. You can pour liquid water into a cup.

Ice is water, too, but it is a **solid**. It is hard. When liquid water gets very, very cold, it becomes solid ice.

A solid is something that has a shape. It does not flow. But when the solid ice gets warm, it melts and turns into liquid again.

Talk with Your Child Talk to your child about the liquids he or she drinks, such as water or milk. Then point out that solids such as popsicles and ice cubes are frozen liquids. Ask your child to point to each picture above and tell you what it shows.

Concept: Solid and liquid are states of matter.

Science

Making Ice Cubes

Marissa decided to make ice cubes. First, she poured water into a tray. She was careful not to spill the water. Water spills because it is a liquid. Then Marissa put the tray into the freezer. Later, the water had turned to ice. It was still water, but it was a solid. Marissa put some ice cubes in a cup and went outside. Soon, the cubes were gone and the cup was filled with water. The ice had melted! The solid water had changed back to a liquid.

Solids and Liquids

Skills: Demonstrate understanding of solids and liquids; Visual discrimination

Answer the question.

Color ☺ for **yes**. Color ☹ for **no**.

1

Is this ice cube a solid?

 yes  no

2

Is this water a liquid?

 yes  no

3

Can water change from solid to liquid?

 yes  no

4

Can water change from liquid to solid?

 yes  no

Solids and Liquids

Skills: Demonstrate understanding of solids and liquids; Visual discrimination; Letter formation; Fine motor skills

Trace the word. Then circle the picture that matches the word.

1 

2 liquid
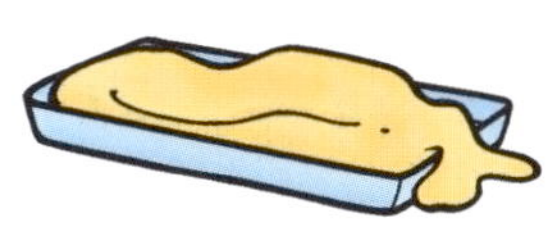
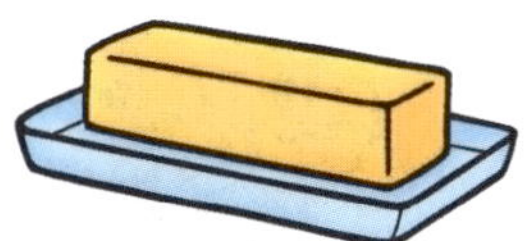

3 melt

4 freeze

Solids and Liquids

Skills: Cause and effect; Comparisons; Visual discrimination; Fine motor skills

Match the pictures to show what happens when things melt.

2

3

4

Solids and Liquids
Stay Cool

Look at the picture and read the story.

STEM

Sebastian's sister is making lemonade for him and his friends. The fresh lemons she is squeezing smell delicious. Soon, his sister will bring out cups and a jug of lemonade full of ice, but Sebastian can't wait. He puts an ice cube in a cup and brings it outside. He sets it on the picnic table and joins his friends to play soccer. Make a tent that will give Sebastian's cup of ice some shade and keep it from melting too quickly.

Stay Cool

STEM Challenge

Objective

Design and construct a tent that will slow down the melting of an ice cube.

Challenge

Place two cups, each with a single ice cube in it, in a sunny location. One cup will be uncovered, and one cup will be covered with a tent.

Suggested Materials

- tape
- popsicle sticks
- playdough
- timer or watch
- paper
- straws

STEM Process

1 Ask

- Is an ice cube liquid water or solid water?
- What can make solid water change to liquid water?
- Can liquid water change to solid water?
- What are some ways to keep solid water from changing to liquid water?

2 Plan

1. Look at the materials you have.
2. In the Plan box on the next page, draw a picture of the tent you will build with the materials.

3 Create

Use the materials to build the tent you drew.

4 Test

1. Put one ice cube in a cup. Place another ice cube in a different cup.
2. Place the cups on a sunny windowsill or in another place they will receive sunlight. Place your tent over one of the cups of ice. Does the tent stay standing?
3. Look in your cups every 5 minutes. In the Test box on the next page, draw what the ice looks like each time you check it.

Stay Cool

Plan

Create: Use materials to build your project.

Test

	5 minutes	10 minutes	15 minutes
Ice with tent			
Ice without tent			

Did it work?

☐ yes ☐ no

Does the Magnet Stick?

Read the text below to explain that a magnet pulls some objects toward it and does not pull others. Then read the science story to your child.

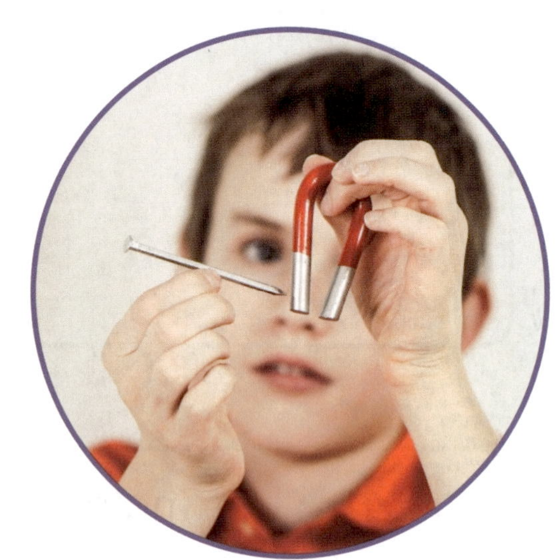

A **magnet** is a kind of metal that **pulls** on other objects.

A magnet will pull and stick to the object if it is made of **metal**.

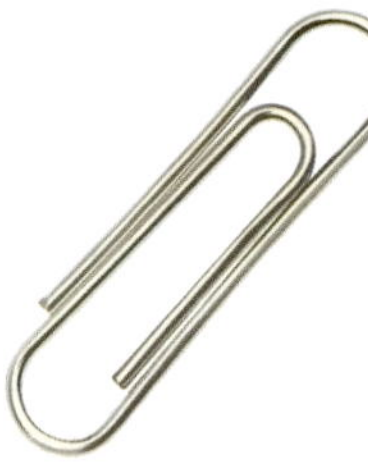

A paper clip is made of metal.

A watch is made of metal.

These objects and other things made of metal will stick to a magnet.

Talk with Your Child Together with your child, look around your home and find objects made of metal. If you have a magnet, use it to see if the objects you've identified as metal stick to the magnet.

Science

Will the Magnet Stick?

Marc has a magnet. He wants to see what will stick to it. First, Marc tries a paper clip. It sticks to the magnet! It is made of metal. Next, he tries a crayon. It does not stick. It is not made of metal. Then he tries his big brother's broken watch. It sticks! It is metal. Last, he tries his favorite toy, Super-Stretch Nick. But Super-Stretch Nick does not stick. Can you guess why? Nick is not metal. A magnet cannot pull on him, but Marc can!

Does the Magnet Stick?

Skills: Demonstrate understanding of magnetic forces on objects; Fine motor skills; Visual discrimination

Look at the picture. Will the object stick to a magnet?

Color ☺ **yes** if the object will stick to a magnet.

Color ☹ **no** if the object will not stick to a magnet.

1

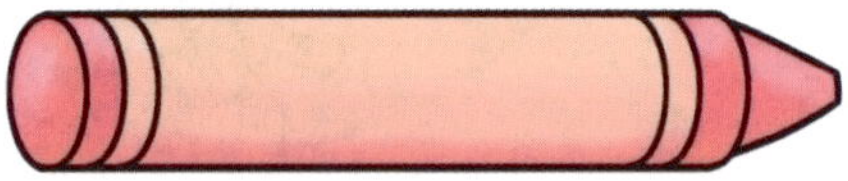

☺ yes ☹ no

2

☺ yes ☹ no

3

☺ yes ☹ no

4

☺ yes ☹ no

Does the Magnet Stick?

Skills: Demonstrate understanding of which objects are probably made of metal; Visual discrimination; Fine motor skills

Look at each row. Circle the object that is made of metal.

2

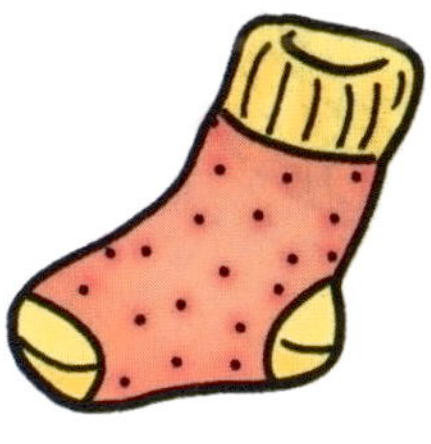

3

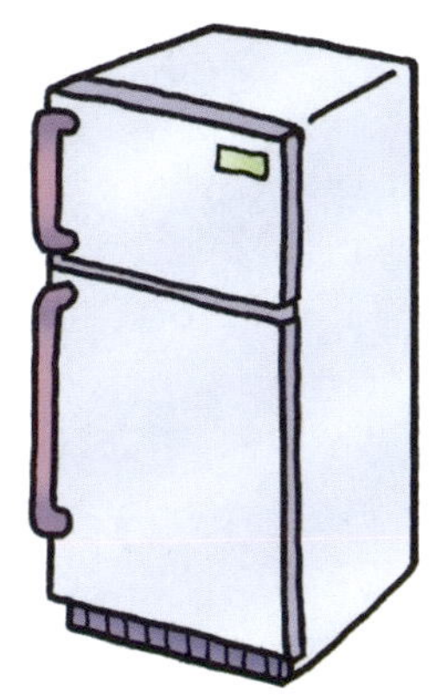

Does the Magnet Stick?

Skills: Demonstrate understanding of magnetic forces on objects; Fine motor skills; Visual discrimination

Will it stick? Draw a line from the object to the magnet if it will stick.

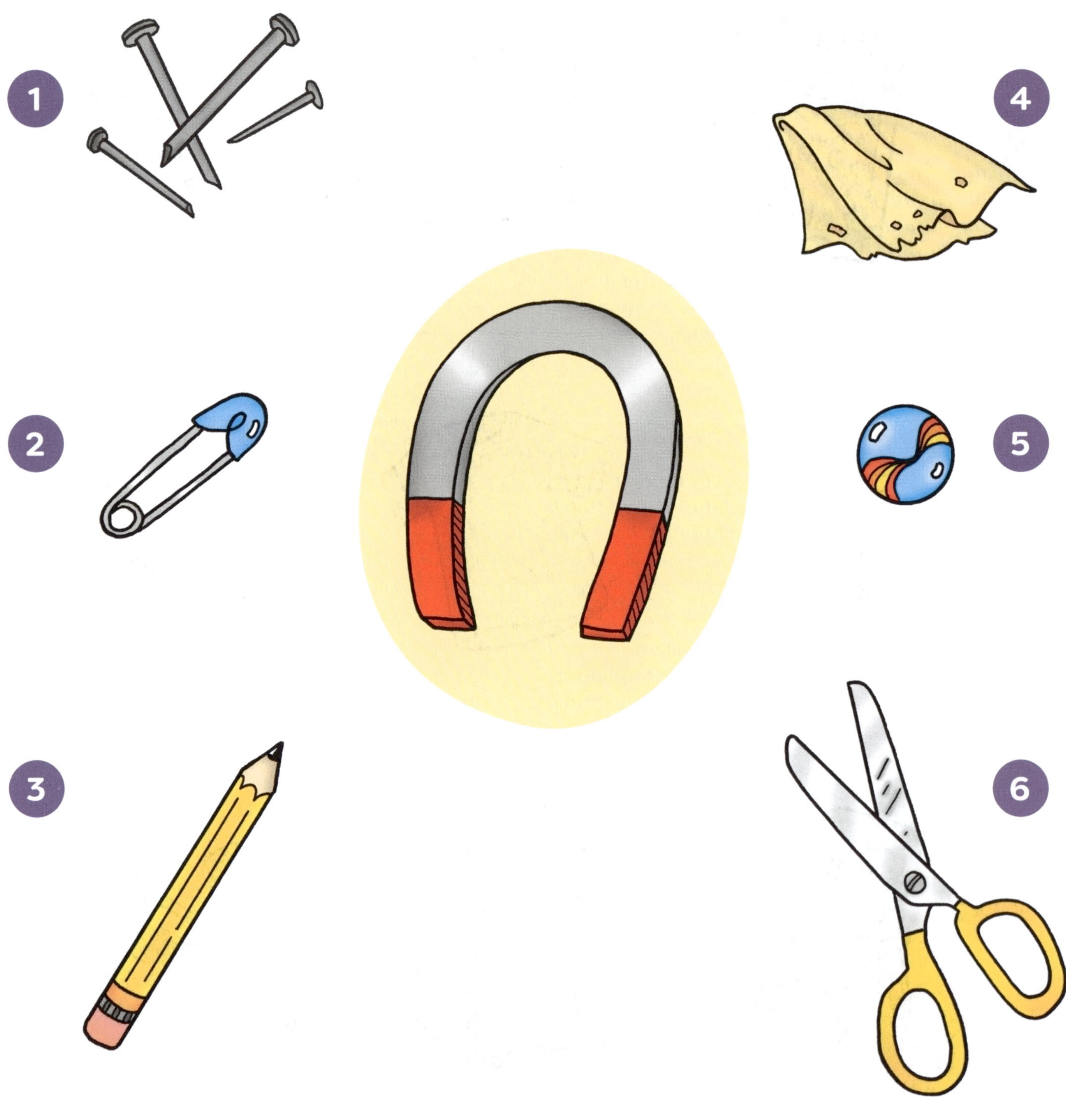

Magnet Painting

STEM Challenge

Look at the picture and read the story.

STEM

Today a magician came to Samar's class. He did many tricks. He even made a coin appear behind Samar's ear! The magician told the class they could do a magic trick, too. He said the trick uses magnets. Magnets seem like magic because they can move metal objects. He gave the students magnets, paper clips, and plates with paint. He asked the students to try to mix the paint without using their hands. Can you help Samar finish the magic trick?

Does the Magnet Stick?

Magnet Painting

STEM Challenge

Objective

Mix two paint colors without touching the paints.

Challenge

- Mix paint without touching it with your hands or a paintbrush
- Magnets must not touch the paints

Suggested Materials

- 2 or more different colors of paint
- paper clip or something metal
- paper plate
- magnet

STEM Process

1 Ask

- What is a magnet?
- What objects stick to magnets?
- How can you mix paint without touching it with your hands?

2 Plan

1. Look at the materials you have.
2. In the Plan box on the next page, draw a picture of how you will mix the paint.

3 Create

Use the materials to start mixing the paints.

4 Test

1. Put two drops of different colors of paint on a paper plate.
2. Put an object made of metal on the plate next to the paint.
3. Try to mix the two colors without touching them. Does it work?
4. In the Test box on the next page, draw a picture to show one thing that happened during the test.

Does the Magnet Stick?

Magnet Painting

Plan

Create: Use materials to build your project.

Test

Did it work? ☐ yes ☐ no

Wheels Do the Work

Read the text below to explain that wheels make work easier for people. Then read the science story to your child.

A car has **wheels** that turn.

A bike and a wagon have wheels, too.

The wheels make it easier to move from place to place.

Wheels make work easier.

Talk with Your Child Look at the pictures with your child. Talk about the things your child uses in his or her own life to make it easier to get from place to place or to move things. Then ask your child to look around your home and point to things that have wheels.

Concept: A wheel and axle is a simple machine that makes work easier.

Helping Dad

One day, Carlos and Gabriel were helping their dad load things into his truck. "Get that big box of newspapers and bring it over here," said their dad. Carlos and Gabriel pushed and pushed the box, but it would hardly move. Then Gabriel had an idea. He got his wagon. The boys asked their dad to lift the box into the wagon. The wagon was easy to pull because it had wheels. "That wagon sure made work easier!" said their dad.

Wheels Do the Work

Skills: Identifying wheels; Visual discrimination

Are the people using wheels to make work easier?

Color ☺ for **yes**. Color ☹ for **no**.

1

 yes  no

2

 yes  no

3

 yes  no

4

yes  no

Wheels Do the Work

Skills: Identifying wheels; Visual discrimination; Fine motor skills

Circle the people who are using wheels to make work easier.

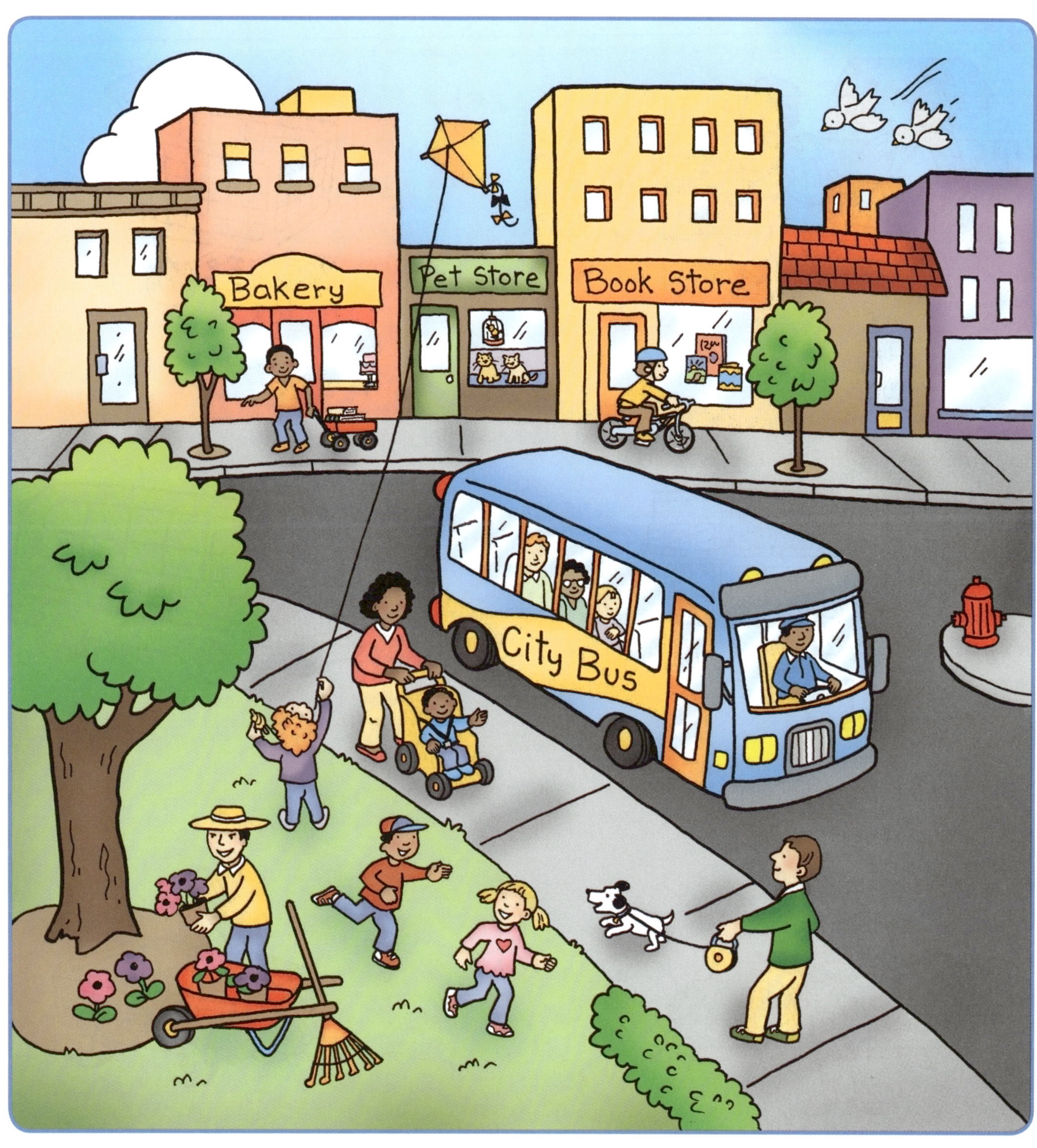

Wheels Do the Work

Skills: Demonstrate understanding that wheels make work easier; Inference; Fine motor skills

Draw a line to show what can help make work easier.

1

2

3

Gumdrop Wheel

STEM Challenge

Look at the picture and read the story.

STEM

Nelly loves to ride her bike. One day, Nelly rode her bike through the park. She rode her bike so fast she didn't see the big rock on the path. Nelly's bike wheel hit the rock and made the tire flat. Help Nelly ride home by building her a new wheel.

Wheels Do the Work

Gumdrop Wheel

STEM Challenge

Objective

Design and construct a wheel.

Challenge

- Use no more than two materials
- Wheel must roll when pushed

Suggested Materials

- gumdrops
- toothpicks
- straws
- mini-marshmallows

STEM Process

1 Ask

- Why does a bike need wheels?
- How do wheels make work easier?
- Which shape is best to make a wheel roll?

2 Plan

1. Look at your materials.
2. In the Plan box on the next page, draw a picture of the wheel you will build.

3 Create

Use the materials to build the wheel you drew.

4 Test

1. Hold your wheel upright.
2. Push the wheel forward to make it roll.
3. Does your wheel roll?
4. In the Test box on the next page, draw a picture to show one thing that happened during the test.

Wheels Do the Work

Gumdrop Wheel

Plan

Create: Use materials to build your project.

Test

Did it work? ☐ yes ☐ no

What Plants Need

Read the text below to explain that plants are living things that need soil, air, water, and sunlight. Then read the science story to your child.

Plants are living things.

Plants need **soil**, **air**, **water**, and **sunlight** to live and grow.

Plants can grow indoors or outdoors in soil or dirt.

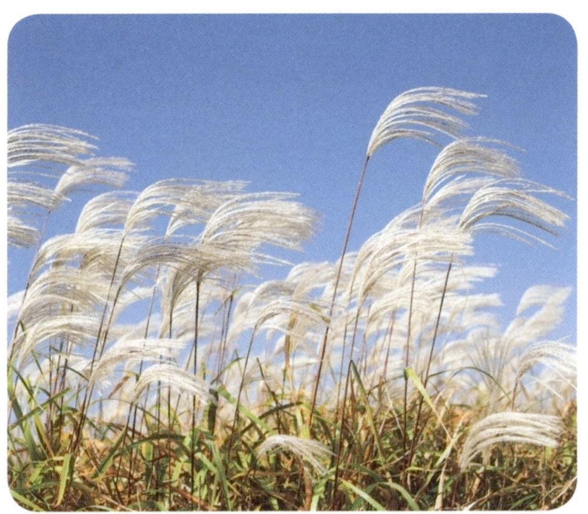

Water helps plants stay healthy. Plants need fresh air and sunlight to be healthy, too.

Talk with Your Child Together with your child, look at the pictures and talk about the things plants need. Then find plants in an indoor or outdoor space and talk about how those plants get the things they need to live.

Concept: Plants are living things that have basic needs.

Science

Three Plants

My friends and I wanted to find out what plants need to live and grow. We gave one plant soil, air, and water, but it did not get sunlight. We gave another plant soil, air, and sunlight, but we didn't water it. We gave the third plant soil, air, water, and sunlight. Guess what happened? The plant without sunlight got droopy and yellow. The plant without water dried up and turned brown. The plant that got everything stayed green and healthy!

What Plants Need

Skills: Demonstrate understanding of what a healthy plant looks like; Visual discrimination

Answer the question.

Color ☺ for **yes**. Color ☹ for **no**.

1

Did this plant get water?

 yes  no

2

Did this plant get water?

 yes  no

3

Did this plant get sunlight?

 yes  no

4

Did this plant have soil?

 yes  no

What Plants Need

Skills: Fine motor skills; Letter formation

Look at the pictures. Then read and trace the words.

What Plants Need

Skills: Demonstrate understanding of what plants need to live; Fine motor skills; Inference

Draw what is missing to show what plants need.
Then draw flowers and color the picture.

What Plants Need

Thirsty Plants

Look at the picture and read the story.

STEM

One hot and sunny afternoon, Ricky and his dad went outside to water the flowers. Ricky tried to water all the plants at the same time. But the hose was only long enough to reach one flowerpot. It is such a hot day, and the plants need water or they will dry up. Help Ricky and his dad water the plants by making something that will water all four plants at once.

What Plants Need

Thirsty Plants

STEM Challenge

Objective

Design and construct a device that will water four plants at one time.

Challenge

- Flowerpots (cups) can be arranged however you like
- Device must water all four plants at the same time

Suggested Materials

- straws
- water
- tape
- glue
- 5 styrofoam cups (4 cups are used to act as flowerpots)

STEM Process

1 Ask

- What do plants need?
- What will happen if a plant does not get water?
- What will happen if a plant gets too much water?

2 Plan

1. Look at the materials you have.
2. In the Plan box on the next page, draw a picture of the watering device you will build with the materials.

3 Create

Use the materials to build the watering can you drew.

4 Test

1. Arrange your four flowerpots (styrofoam cups).
2. Put your watering device on or near the plants.
3. Pour water in the device. Does it give water to all four plants?
4. In the Test box on the next page, draw a picture to show one thing that happened during the test.

Thirsty Plants

Plan

Create: Use materials to build your project.

Test

Did it work? ☐ yes ☐ no

What Animals Need

Read the text below to explain that animals are living things that need food, water, air, and shelter. Then read the science story to your child.

Pets are animals. Animals are living things.

Animals need four things to live and grow: **food**, **water**, **air**, and **shelter**.

Shelter is a place where animals can go to be safe from weather or danger.

Our homes give our pets shelter. Wild animals find shelter in trees, under rocks, and in the ground.

Talk with Your Child Look at the pictures with your child. Talk about the different types of food and shelter that different animals need to live and grow. Then talk about how pets get water and how wild animals might get water.

Concept: Animals are living things that have basic needs.

Science

Classroom Pet

Animals are living things. They need food, water, air, and shelter to live and grow. Our class pet, Miss Bunny, needs all those things. A wild rabbit finds its own food, water, and shelter. But Miss Bunny is a pet. We give her fresh hay and carrots. We give her clean water, too. A wild rabbit has a cozy hole in the ground for shelter. Miss Bunny has a cage in our classroom's quiet corner.

What Animals Need

Skills: Demonstrate understanding of animals' basic needs; Visual discrimination

Answer the question.

Color ☺ for **yes**. Color  for **no**.

1

Does a rabbit need food?

 yes  no

2

Does a rabbit need shelter?

 yes  no

3

Is this a safe place for a rabbit to live?

 yes  no

4

Does a rabbit need fresh air?

 yes  no

What Animals Need

Skills: Letter formation; Fine motor skills

Trace the words. Then color the pictures.

What Animals Need

Skills: Demonstrate understanding of living things' shelters; Visual discrimination; Fine motor skills

Draw a line to match the living thing with a safe place to live.

 • • 

 • • 

3

 • • 

4

 • • 

Bunny Cage

STEM Challenge

Look at the picture and read the story.

STEM

Luna's mom came home with a surprise for Luna. "What is in the box?" Luna asked her mom. "Take a look and see," replied Luna's mom. Luna opened the box and saw a bunny! She was happy to have a new pet, but Luna did not know how to take care of a bunny. "Animals need food, water, air, and shelter," said Luna's mom. "I will give it some food and water, but we will need shelter for it." Can you make a bunny cage for Luna's pet?

What Animals Need

Bunny Cage

STEM Challenge

Objective

Design and construct a bunny cage.

Challenge

- Use only the suggested materials
- Cage must be at least one marker tall and one marker wide
- Cage must have holes for fresh air to flow through

Suggested Materials

- marshmallows
- toothpicks

STEM Process

1 Ask

- What do animals need to live and grow?
- What is shelter?
- Why should the bunny cage have holes?

2 Plan

1. Look at the materials you have.
2. In the Plan box on the next page, draw a picture of the cage you will build.

3 Create

Use the materials to build the cage you drew.

4 Test

1. Measure your cage. Is it at least one marker tall?
2. Place a toy in the cage. Is it big enough to hold the toy? Does it have holes so a bunny can get fresh air?
3. In the Test box on the next page, draw a picture to show one thing that happened during the test.

Bunny Cage

Plan

Create: Use materials to build your project.

Test

Did it work? ☐ yes ☐ no

I'm Growing!

Read the text below to explain that people change and grow. Then read the science story to your child.

People can **grow** and **change**.

As you grow, your body gets bigger. As you grow, you can do more things.

When you are a baby, you can crawl. Then you grow older and can walk. After you grow some more, you can run and jump.

A baby changes and grows into a young child. A child grows into a teenager, and a teenager grows into an adult.

Talk with Your Child Have your child look at the pictures on the next page. Explain that the picture under "Then" shows how tall the girl was as a baby. The picture under "Now" shows how the girl changed and grew. Then ask the questions: What are some ways that people grow and change? Discuss some of the things your child does now that he or she could not do when he or she was a baby.

Baby to Big Kid

My name is Mia. In school, I learned that living things grow and change. A long time ago, I was a baby. Now I am five years old, and I have grown. When I was younger, I crawled, and then I learned to walk. Now that I am five, I can run fast, and I even know how to ride a bike! My mom says she remembers when I was only two feet tall. Now, I'm three feet tall. I'm growing into a big kid!

I'm Growing!

Skills: Visual discrimination; Inference

Answer the question.

Color (smiley face) for **yes**. Color (frowning face) for **no**.

1

Do both of them have teeth?

 yes  no

2

Is the girl taller than the baby?

 yes  no

3

Can the baby and the girl ride a bike?

 yes  no

4

Do both the girl and the baby need to be carried?

 yes  no

I'm Growing!

Skills: Demonstrate understanding of how people grow and change; Inference; Fine motor skills

Draw a line to match then and now.

I'm Growing!

Skills: Visual discrimination; Sequencing; Fine motor skills; Inference

Draw a line to show the order in which people grow.

 • • 

• • 2

 • • 3

 • • 

I'm Growing!
Big Kid Bed

STEM Challenge

Look at the picture and read the story.

STEM

My name is Jasper, and I need your help! When I was a baby, I slept in a crib at night. But now my body has changed. I am taller, and I weigh more. I am a big kid now! Can you help build a bed that won't break when I lie down on it?

I'm Growing!

Big Kid Bed

STEM Challenge

Objective

Design and construct a bed that can hold a toy.

Challenge

- Bed must hold a stuffed animal, baby doll, or other toy for at least 15 seconds
- Bed must be lifted off the ground by at least 2 inches

Suggested Materials

- tape
- glue
- paper
- shoe box
- paper towel rolls
- stuffed animal, baby doll, or other toy

STEM Process

1 Ask

- What are some reasons a child would need a new bed?
- What shape is a bed?
- How heavy is a stuffed animal?

2 Plan

1. Look at the materials you have.
2. In the Plan box on the next page, draw a picture of the bed you will build with the materials.

3 Create

Use the materials to build the bed you drew.

4 Test

1. Place your stuffed animal, baby doll, or other toy on the bed. Does the toy fit? Is the bed at least one pink eraser high?
2. Count to 15 seconds. Does the bed stay standing?
3. In the Test box on the next page, draw a picture to show one thing that happened during the test.

I'm Growing!

Big Kid Bed

STEM Journal

Plan

Create: Use materials to build your project.

Test

Did it work? ☐ yes ☐ no

Trees Have Parts

Read the text below to explain that trees are plants that have parts that help them live and grow. Then read the science story to your child.

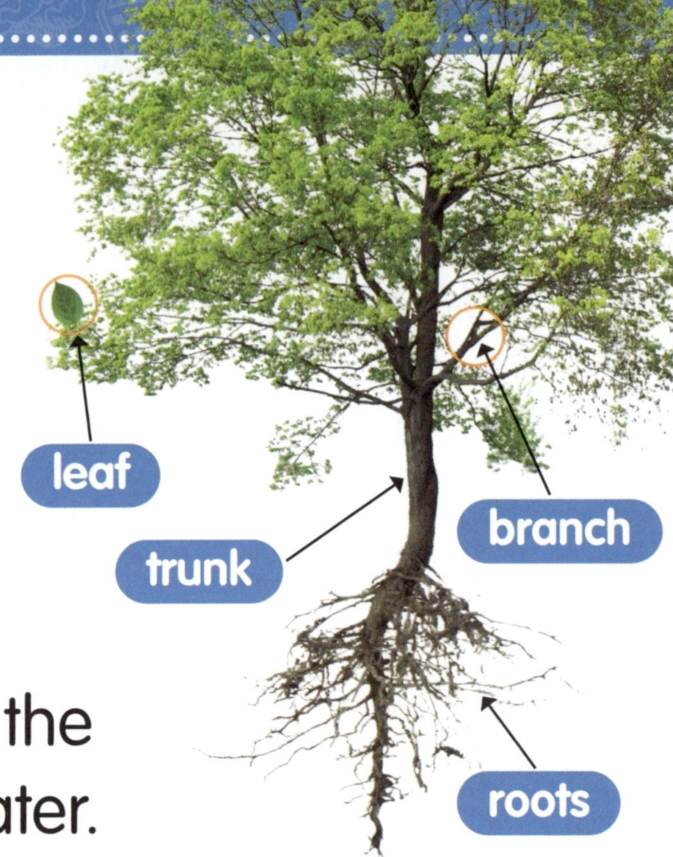

Trees are **plants**. Plants have parts that help them live and grow.

The **roots** stretch under the ground and soak up water.

The **trunk** is the thick part of the tree that carries water to the branches and leaves.

A **branch** stretches far out of the trunk and grows **leaves** that make food for the tree.

Some **fruits** have **seeds** inside them that help grow more trees.

Talk with Your Child Together with your child, point to the tree and name its parts.

Apple Trees

Olivia's class went on a field trip to an apple farm. The farmer told Olivia's class that an apple tree has parts that help it grow and stay healthy. The roots take in water from the soil. The trunk carries the water up to the leaves. The leaves make food for the tree to help it grow. Then the tree starts to grow apples. The apples have seeds inside them. The farmer cut open an apple and told them that if they plant the seeds, they will grow into apple trees!

Trees Have Parts

Skills: Demonstrate understanding of the parts of a plant; Visual discrimination

Answer the question.

Color ☺ for **yes**. Color ☹ for **no**.

1

Does this tree have roots?

 yes  no

2

Does this tree have leaves?

 yes  no

3

Can you pick apples and eat them?

 yes  no

4

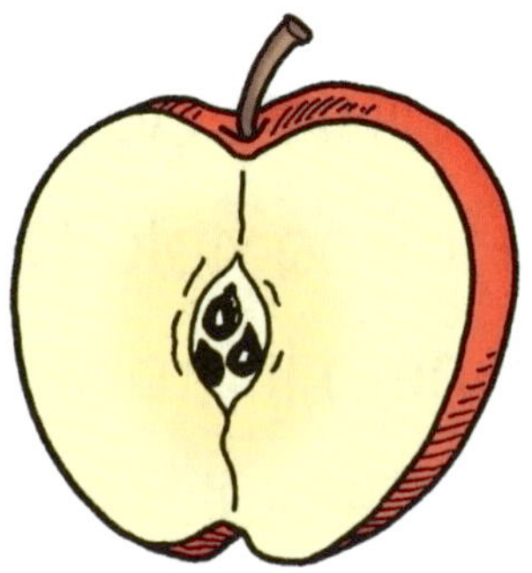

Can apple seeds grow into apple trees if you plant them?

 yes  no

Trees Have Parts

Skills: Demonstrate understanding of the parts of a plant; Letter formation; Visual discrimination; Fine motor skills

Trace. Then draw a line to the correct part in the pictures.

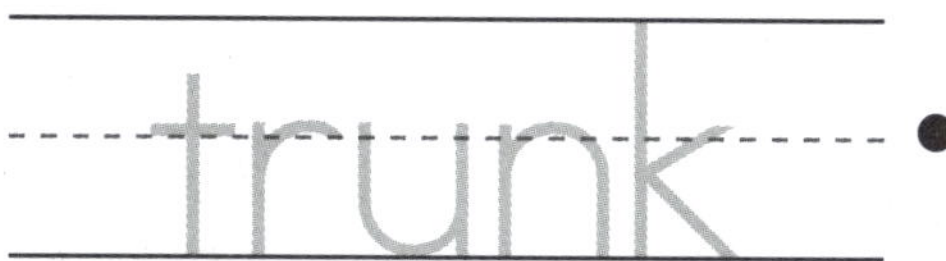

3

4

Trees Have Parts

Skills: Making connections; Inference; Categorizing

Look at the first picture. Then circle the picture that does not belong.

2

3

4

  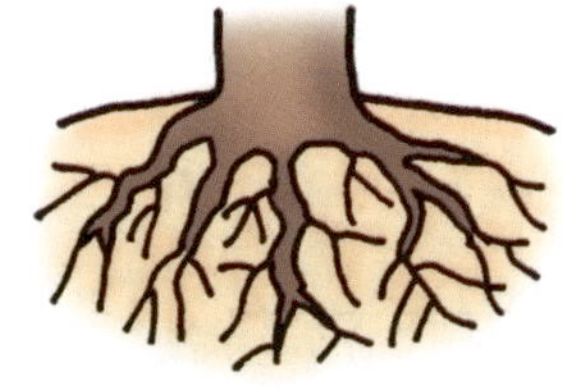 

Tall Apple Tree

Look at the picture and read the story.

STEM

The people from Tree Town wish they had more apple trees. They will plant seeds in good soil in a sunny place. They will water the trees so that they grow. But that will take so long! They want a tall apple tree with at least one apple right now! Can you make them a tall apple tree that has one apple at the very top?

Tall Apple Tree

STEM Challenge

Objective

Design and construct a tall tree that will hold one apple at the top.

Challenge

- Must stop building tree after 30 seconds
- Must place apple on the top of the tree
- Tree must stay standing for 10 seconds while an apple is on top

Suggested Materials

- 25 plastic cups
- apple
- timer or stopwatch

STEM Process

1 Ask

- What are the parts of a tree?
- What part of the tree does an apple grow on?
- How can you stack cups up high while keeping a sturdy base?

2 Plan

1. Look at the materials you have.
2. In the Plan box on the next page, draw a picture of the tree you will build with the materials.

3 Create

Use the materials to build the tree you drew.

4 Test

1. Start your timer.
2. Use the plastic cups to build the tallest tree you can in 30 seconds.
3. When the timer stops, place an apple on the top of the tree. Count to 10 seconds. Does the tree stay standing?
4. In the Test box on the next page, draw a picture to show one thing that happened during the test.

Tall Apple Tree

Plan

Create: Use materials to build your project.

Test

How tall was your tree?

________ cup(s)

How wide was your tree?

________ cup(s)

Did your apple fall? ☐ yes ☐ no

Animals Have Parts

Read the text below to explain that animals are living things that have parts that help them live. Then read the science story to your child.

Animals are living things. Animals have parts that help them live.

Some animals have **fur** to keep them warm, and some animals have **feathers** to help them **fly**.

Some animals have **scales** to protect them from water or rough ground, and some have **webbed feet** to help them swim.

Some animals have **legs** and **feet** to help them run and climb, and some animals do not have any legs at all!

Talk with Your Child Have your child point to and name the animals above. Discuss what unique parts and coverings the animals have and how the body parts or coverings help the animals live and grow. Then ask your child to look at the pictures and tell you which body parts the animals have in common.

Concept: Animals have parts that help them live.

Science

Animals at the Zoo

At the zoo, Jake saw all kinds of animals. He saw a bear with thick fur that kept it warm. It walked on four legs and had sharp claws for climbing. Jake saw a crocodile covered with scales. It used its tail and webbed feet to zoom through the water. And its four legs made it fast on land, too. By the pond, Jake saw ducks. They had feathers to keep them warm and to help them fly. They also had webbed feet to help them swim.

Animals Have Parts

Skills: Demonstrate understanding of animal coverings and body parts; Visual discrimination

Look at the pictures. Answer the questions.

Color  for **yes**. Color ☹ for **no**.

1

Do both animals have fur?

 yes  no

2

Do both animals have scales?

 yes  no

3

Does a bear have sharp claws for climbing?

 yes  no

4

Does a duck have webbed feet for swimming?

 yes  no

Animals Have Parts

Skills: Demonstrate understanding of animal coverings and body parts; Visual discrimination; Inference; Fine motor skills

Draw a line to match the feet with the body.

4

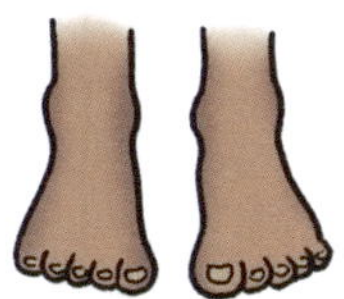

Animals Have Parts

Skills: Demonstrate understanding of animal coverings and body parts; Visual discrimination; Colors

Color the animal (green crayon) that has feathers and can fly.

Color the animal (yellow crayon) that has fur and sharp claws.

Color the animal (gray crayon) that has a long nose and big ears.

Color the animal (orange crayon) that has a long neck and spotted fur.

Color the animals (red crayon) that do not have legs.

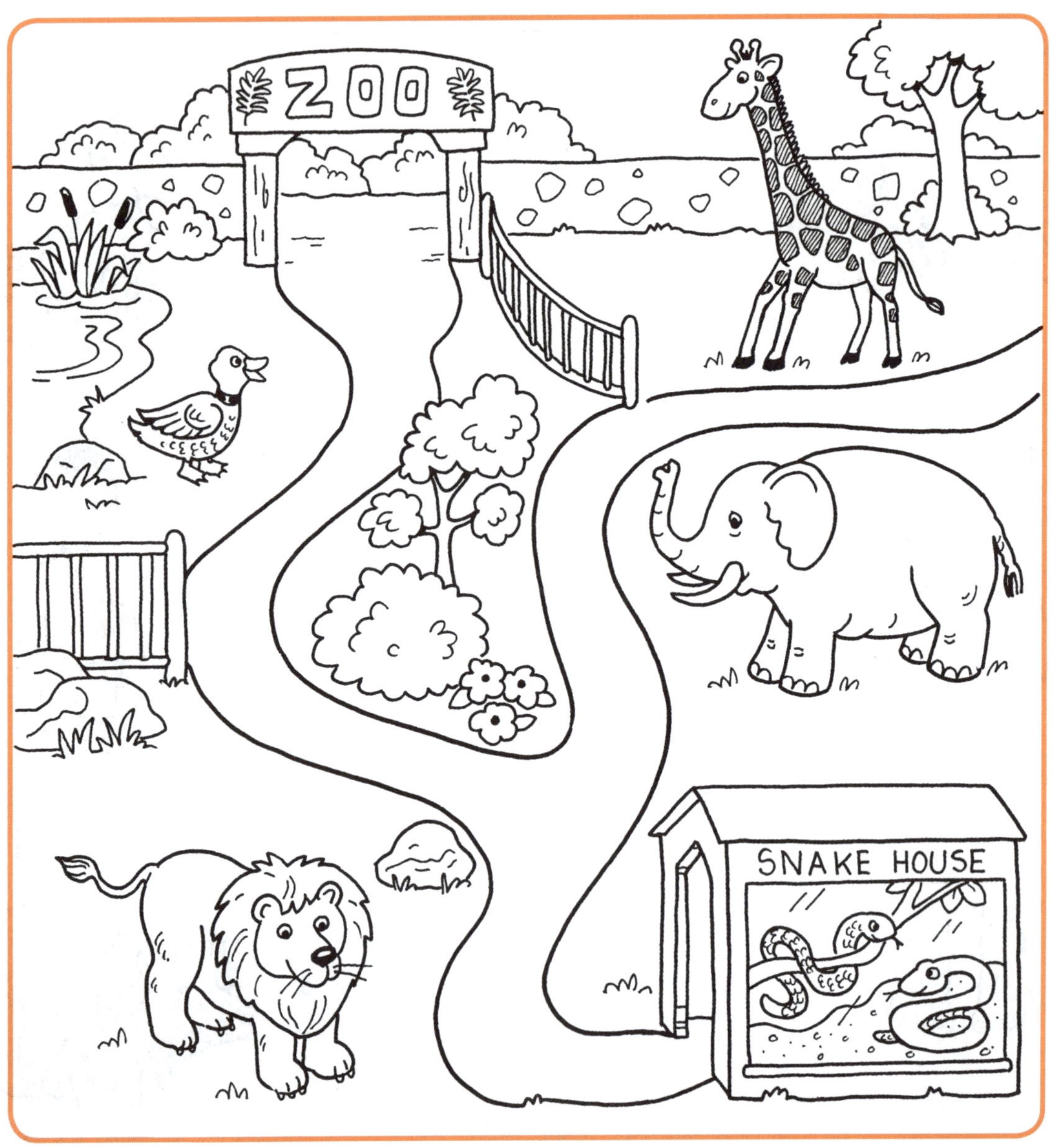

Animals Have Parts

Animal Footprints

STEM Challenge

Look at the picture and read the story.

STEM

Deep in the woods, there is a magical fruit tree that grows the yummiest fruits. A grumpy elf lives near the magical fruit tree. It likes to scare off people who try to walk in the forest and pick the fruit. The grumpy elf will only let animals eat the fruit from the magical tree. Trick the grumpy elf by making a pair of shoes that look like an animal's foot so that it will leave animal footprints behind. This will keep you safe from the grumpy elf.

Animals Have Parts
Animal Footprints

STEM Challenge

Objective

Design and construct a pair of shoes that resemble an animal's foot.

Challenge

- Must be able to walk 10 steps in shoes
- Shoes must have claws, webbed feet, or a similar animal covering to the animal you chose

Suggested Materials

- scissors
- tape
- stapler
- paper
- cardboard
- rubber bands
- 2 empty tissue boxes

STEM Process

1 Ask

- What body parts does the animal you chose have?
- What special covering does the animal have?
- How does the animal move?

2 Plan

1. Look at the materials you have.
2. In the Plan box on the next page, draw a picture of the shoes you will build with the materials.

3 Create

Use the materials to build the shoes you drew.

4 Test

1. Put your feet inside the shoes. Do your feet fit inside the shoes? Do your shoes have the same parts or covering as the animal you chose?
2. Walk 10 steps. Do your feet stay in the shoes? Do your shoes fall apart?
3. In the Test box on the next page, draw a picture to show one thing that happened during the test.

Animal Footprints

Plan

Create: Use materials to build your project.

Test

Did it work? ☐ yes ☐ no

From Egg to Frog

Read the text below to explain that frogs are living things that change and grow. Then read the science story to your child.

A frog is a living thing.
Living things change and grow.

First, a mother frog lays **eggs** in the water.

Next, a **tadpole** pushes out of each egg.

Then, the tadpole grows legs and turns into a **froglet**.

Finally, a froglet loses its tail and changes into an adult **frog**.

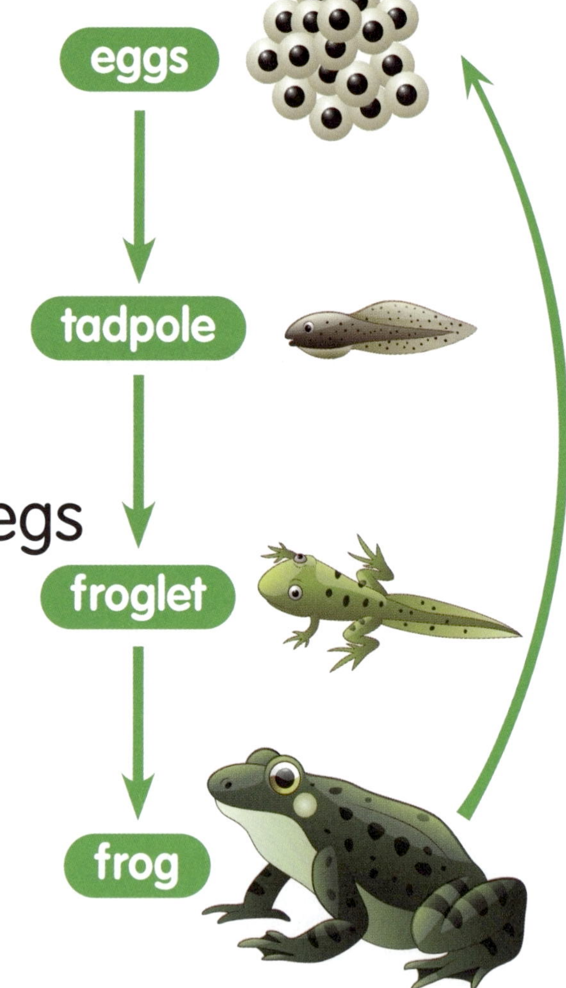

Talk with Your Child Look at the pictures above and have your child point to the frog eggs, tadpole, froglet, and frog. Then discuss the changes that happen as a frog grows. Remind your child that frogs are living things, like people, and living things can change and grow.

Concept: Living things change and grow.

Frogs Change and Grow

My mom read me a book about frogs. It said that frogs start out as tiny eggs. The mother frog lays her eggs in water. Soon, babies called tadpoles push out of the eggs. Tadpoles have a tail, but no legs. They can breathe underwater, but not on land. First tadpoles grow back legs, then front legs. Their tail gets shorter, and they turn into froglets. Lungs grow inside them so they can breathe on land. Before long, the froglets change into frogs.

From Egg to Frog

Skills: Demonstrate understanding of a frog's body parts; Visual discrimination

Answer the question.

Color ☺ for **yes**. Color ☹ for **no**.

1

Does a mother frog lay eggs in water?

 yes  no

2

Does a tadpole have legs?

 yes  no

3

Does a froglet have legs and a tail?

 yes  no

4

Does this picture show a frog?

 yes  no

From Egg to Frog

Skills: Letter formation; Picture and word meaning

Trace. Then point to the picture and say the word.

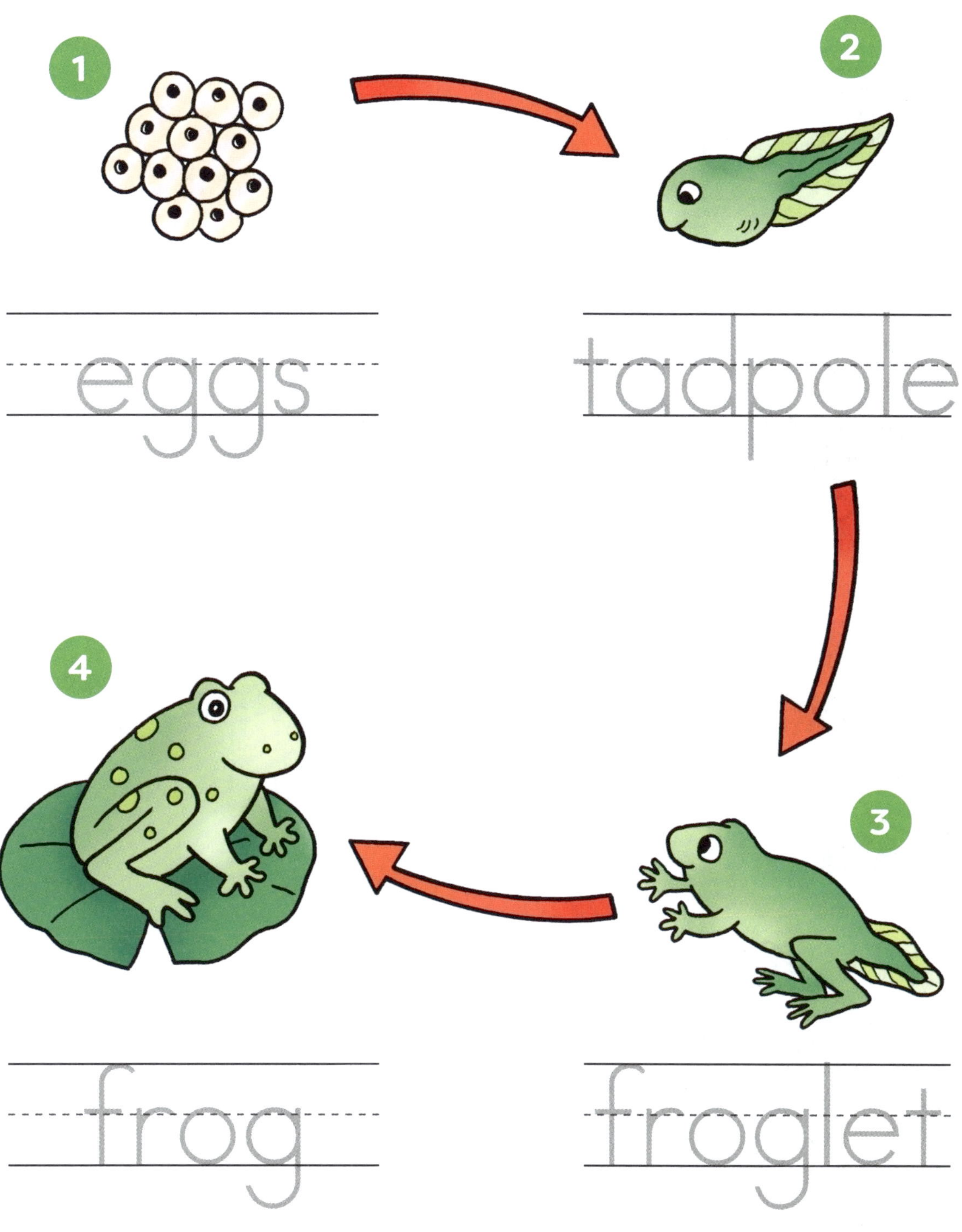

From Egg to Frog

Skills: Demonstrate understanding of a frog's lifecycle; Sequencing; Visual discrimination

Draw a line from the picture to the number to show how a frog grows.

 •  • 1

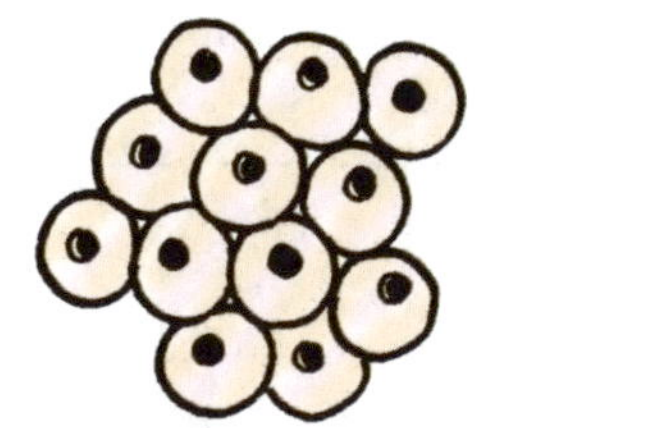 • • 2

 • • 3

 • • 4

Lily Pad

Look at the picture and read the story.

STEM

Miss Frog put on her favorite dress. She is on her way to visit her friend Miss Duck in the pond. A new baby tadpole just pushed out of an egg, and Miss Frog wants to tell Miss Duck all about it. But the pond does not have any lily pads to stand on, and she does not want to get her dress wet. Help Miss Frog visit her friend by making her a lily pad she can float on.

From Egg to Frog

Lily Pad

STEM Challenge

Objective

Design and construct a lily pad that will hold a "frog."

Challenge

- Lily pad must float
- Lily pad must be strong enough to hold a "frog," or 22 pennies

Suggested Materials

- tape
- string
- straws
- aluminum foil
- tub or bucket
- pennies (22)
- water
- glue
- tape

STEM Process

1 Ask

- What makes something sink?
- Which materials float?
- Can a frog egg, tadpole, or froglet sit on a lily pad?

2 Plan

1. Look at the materials you have.
2. In the Plan box on the next page, draw a picture of the lily pad you will build with the materials

3 Create

Use the materials to build the lily pad you drew.

4 Test

1. Put your lily pad in a tub or bucket of water. Does your lily pad float or sink?
2. Place your "frog" (pennies) on the lily pad. Does your lily pad stay above the water?
3. In the Test box on the next page, draw a picture to show one thing that happened during the test.

Lily Pad

Plan

Create: Use materials to build your project.

Test

Did it work? ☐ yes ☐ no

Dinosaurs

Read the text below to explain that dinosaurs were living things that once lived on Earth. Then read the science story to your child.

A long time ago, **dinosaurs** lived on Earth. Some dinosaurs were big, and some were small.

Some dinosaurs walked on four legs, and some walked on two. Some dinosaurs swam, and some dinosaurs flew.

Old **fossils**, or dinosaur bones, can be found deep in the Earth's crust. Studying fossils helps us learn more about dinosaurs.

Talk with Your Child Together with your child, look at the pictures and point to the dinosaurs. Ask your child questions such as, "Do dinosaurs still live on Earth? Were they big or small? Could some dinosaurs fly or swim? What can you learn from dinosaur fossils?"

Concept: Dinosaurs were living things that once lived on Earth.

Science

Trip to the Museum

Zoe and her brother Zack went to the museum. "Look at this big animal!" said Zoe. "That's a dinosaur," said Zack. "They lived a long time ago. They hatched from eggs. Some dinosaurs were as tall as houses, and some were as small as dogs. Dinosaurs swam, flew, or walked," explained Zack. "But Zack, how do we know about dinosaurs?" asked Zoe. "We find old dinosaur bones in the Earth, and they help us learn more," replied Zack.

Dinosaurs

Skills: Visual discrimination; Inference

Answer the question.

Color ☺ for **yes**. Color  for **no**.

Did some dinosaurs fly?

 **yes**  **no**

2

Were all dinosaurs big?

 **yes**  **no**

3

Do fossils tell us the size and shape of dinosaurs?

 **yes**  **no**

Are there dinosaurs living today?

 **yes**  **no**

Dinosaurs

Skills: Visual discrimination; Comparing; Fine motor skills

Look at the pictures in the row. Circle the one that is the **smallest**.

2

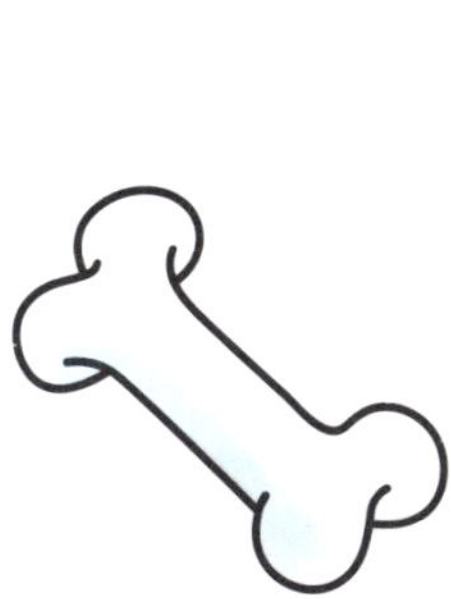
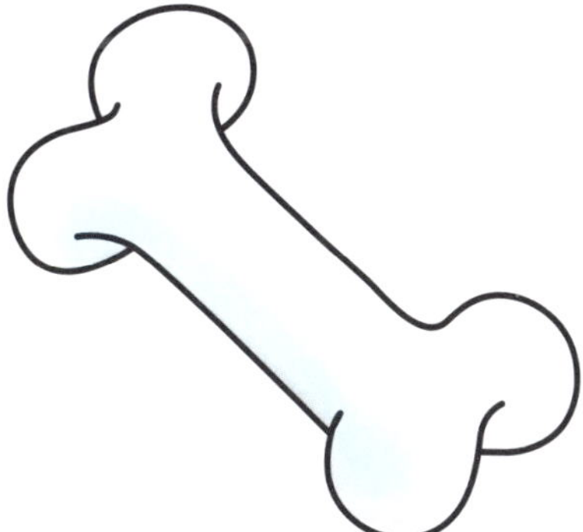
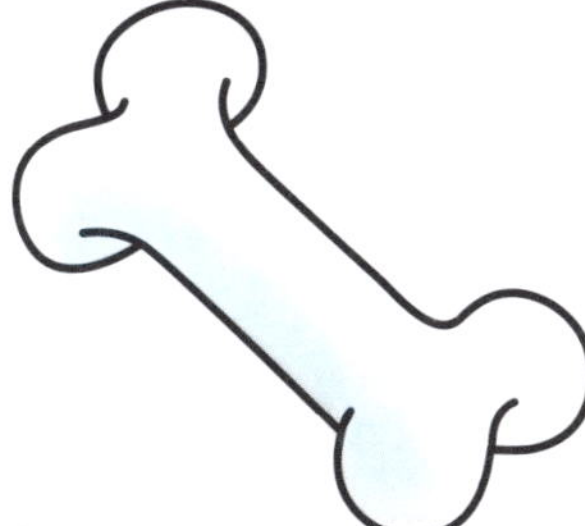

3

Dinosaurs

Skills: Visual discrimination; Fine motor skills

Draw a line to match each fossil with its dinosaur.

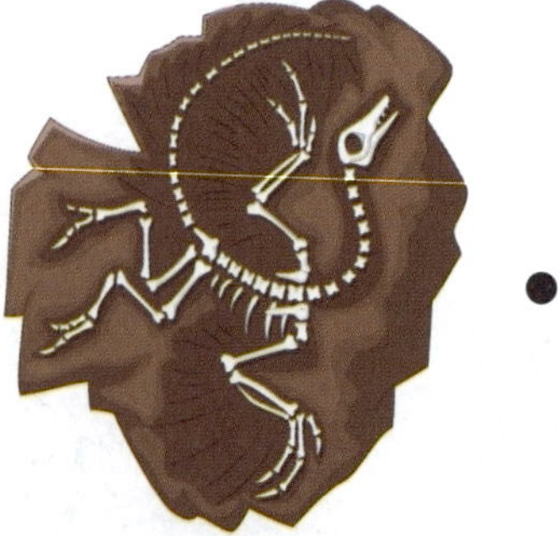

Dino Fossils

Look at the picture and read the story.

STEM

Emerson is looking for a dinosaur fossil. He digs all day until finally, he hits something. Emerson takes a brush and wipes away the dirt. It's a fossil! Emerson grabs the bones and wonders what kind of dinosaur the fossils belong to. Help Emerson by putting together the fossils to make a model of the dinosaur.

Dino Fossils

STEM Challenge

Objective

Find and choose a picture of a dinosaur. Then design and construct a model of that dinosaur.

Challenge

- Only two materials should be used to construct the dinosaur
- The dinosaur must have a head, a tail, and the same number of legs as the dinosaur in the picture you chose

Suggested Materials

- gumdrops
- bendable straws
- clay or putty
- wood skewers

STEM Process

1 Ask

- What are the body parts of a dinosaur?
- Where can you find a picture of a dinosaur?
- What is the name of the dinosaur you would like to construct?

2 Plan

1. Look at the materials you have.
2. In the Plan box on the next page, draw a picture of the dinosaur you will build with the materials.

3 Create

Use the materials to build the dinosaur you drew.

4 Test

1. Place your constructed dinosaur next to the picture of the dinosaur you chose. Does it have the same body parts?
2. Does your dinosaur stay together if you pick it up?
3. In the Test box on the next page, draw a picture to show one thing that happened during the test.

Dino Fossils

Plan

Create: Use materials to build your project.

Test

Did it work? ☐ yes ☐ no

Four Seasons

Read the text below to explain that changes in weather occur from day to day and across seasons. These changes affect Earth and its people. Then read the science story to your child.

Earth is like a big ball that moves around the sun. As Earth moves, the **seasons** change.

The Earth has four seasons: **spring**, **summer**, **fall**, and **winter**. The weather changes from season to season.

Talk with Your Child Have your child point to the pictures in order and name the seasons: spring, summer, fall, and winter. Ask your child to point to the season it is now and ask what season is next. Discuss the weather and the clothes your child might wear in each season. Lastly, ask your child what season he or she likes the most, and why.

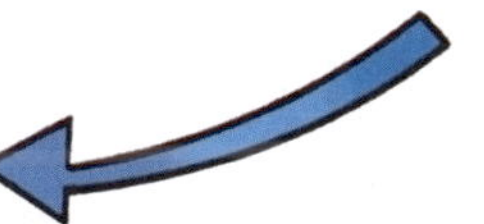

The Seasons and Ava's Tree

In spring, the tree outside Ava's window has tiny, new green leaves. She sees baby birds in their nest. When summer comes, the tree has big green leaves. Ava sits in the shade of the tree and reads a book. When fall comes, the leaves on the tree turn yellow, orange, and red before they fall to the ground. Finally, in winter, the branches of the tree are bare. Snow is everywhere, but not for long! The seasons will change again soon.

Four Seasons

Skills: Demonstrate understanding of weather changes during the four seasons; Visual discrimination; Fine motor skills

Read the word. Look at the pictures.
Then circle the picture that matches the word.

1 spring

2 summer

3 fall

4 winter

Four Seasons

Skills: Demonstrate understanding of weather changes during the four seasons; Visual discrimination; Fine motor skills; Sequencing

Number the pictures to show the order of the seasons.

Four Seasons

Skills: Letter formation; Demonstrate understanding of weather changes during the four seasons; Fine motor skills

Trace the word. Then draw a line to match the word with the picture.

1. 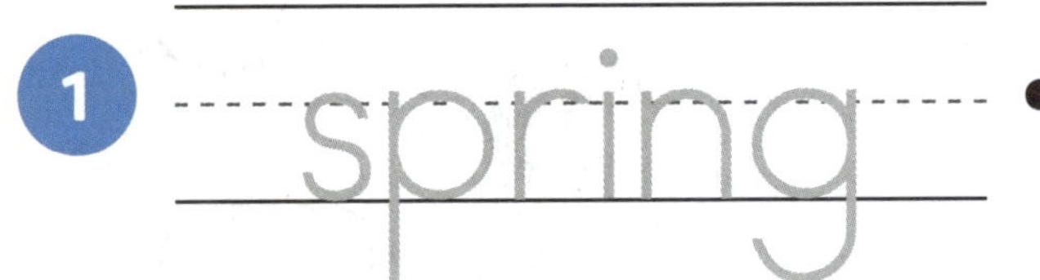

2. 

3. 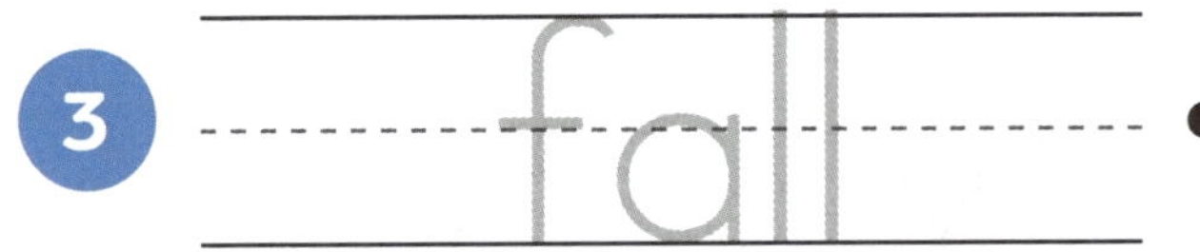

4. 

Leaky Roof

STEM Challenge

Look at the picture and read the story.

STEM

One spring afternoon, Penny was outside picking flowers. She had just put the flowers into a vase when the clouds turned gray, and it started to rain. Penny rushed inside her house, where it was warm and dry. Suddenly, Penny heard a "drip, drop." Penny looked all around until finally, she looked up, and a drop of water fell on her head. "Oh no! There's a leak in the roof!" Help Penny stay dry by building her a house with a roof that doesn't leak.

Leaky Roof

Objective

Design and construct a house with a working roof.

Challenge

- House must stand upright for at least 15 seconds
- Roof must keep dripping water from leaking through for 15 seconds

Suggested Materials

- popsicle sticks
- wax paper
- aluminum foil
- tape
- glue
- water

STEM Process

1 Ask

- In what season does it rain the most where you live?
- What shape is your house?
- What material will not soak up water?

2 Plan

1. Look at the materials you have.
2. In the Plan box on the next page, draw a picture of the house you will build.

3 Create

Use the materials to build the house you drew.

4 Test

1. Stand your house upright.
2. Drip water over the roof for 15 seconds. Is your house still standing? Does water leak through your roof?
3. In the Test box on the next page, draw a picture to show one thing that happened during the test.

Four Seasons

Leaky Roof

STEM Journal

Plan

Create: Use materials to build your project.

Test

Did it work? ☐ yes ☐ no

Bodies of Water

Read the text below to explain that Earth is mostly covered by different bodies of water. Then read the science story to your child.

Most of Earth is covered by **water**.
There are many types, or **bodies**, of water.
There are oceans, rivers, lakes, and ponds.

A **pond** is a small body of water.

A **lake** is bigger than a pond. A lake has land all around it.

A **river** is a long, narrow body of water that flows to a lake or an ocean.

An **ocean** is the biggest body of water.

Talk with Your Child Discuss the differences between each body of water (pond, lake, river, or ocean). Talk with your child about a body of water your child has seen. Ask him or her to tell about the activities he or she can do at each body of water (sail a boat, swim, whale watching, etc.).

Concept: Most of Earth is covered by water.

Science

Bodies of Water Everywhere

My family visits many places during the summer. That's how I found out that most of Earth is covered by water. Earth has oceans, rivers, lakes, and ponds. My uncle's horses drink from a small body of water called a pond. Last summer, my family sailed a boat on a lake. Then we rode our bikes over a bridge across a river. Once I watched whales splash in the ocean. I wonder what bodies of water I'll see next summer!

Bodies of Water

Skills: Demonstrate understanding of bodies of water; Visual discrimination

Answer the question.

Color ☺ for **yes**. Color  for **no**.

1

Is a pond bigger than a lake?

 **yes**  **no**

2

Is there land all around a lake?

 **yes**  **no**

3

Can a river flow from a lake to an ocean?

 **yes**  **no**

4

Is an ocean bigger than a lake?

 **yes**  **no**

Bodies of Water

Skills: Visual discrimination; Letter formation; Word and picture meaning

Color the bodies of water blue.
Then read the sentence and trace the word.

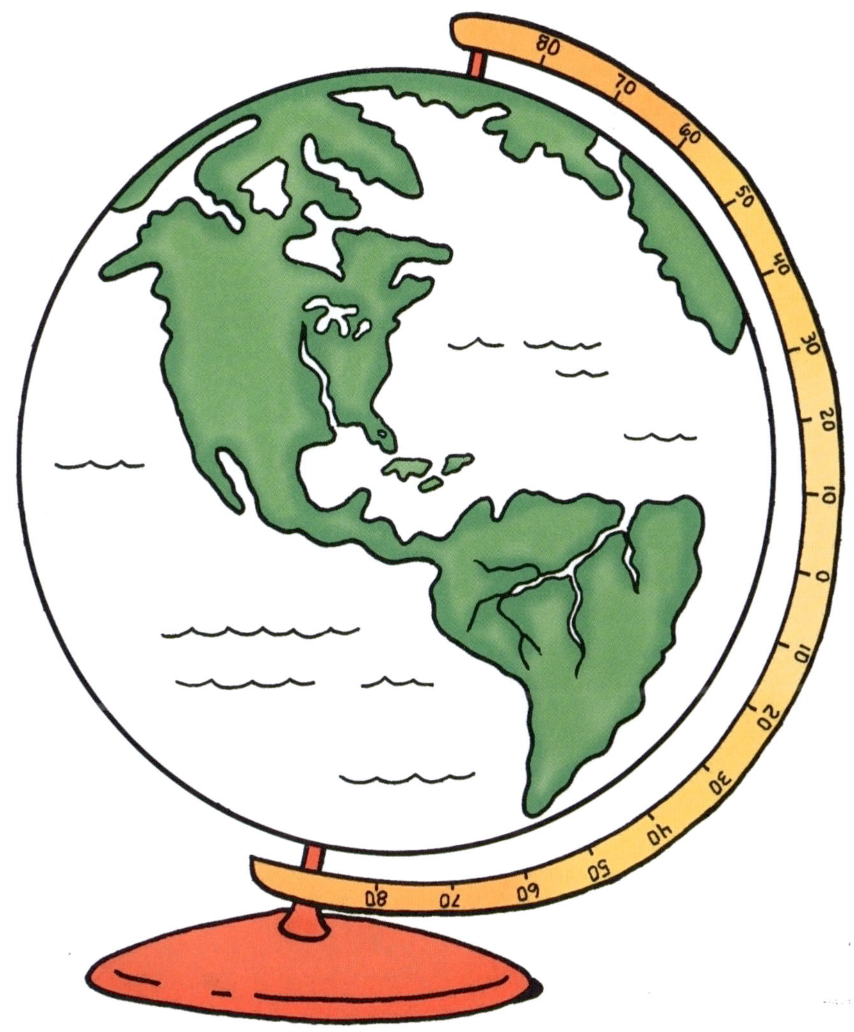

Earth has land and

water.

Bodies of Water

Skills: Demonstrate understanding of bodies of water; Letter formation; Word and picture meaning

Trace. Then draw a line to match the word to the picture.

Crocodile Lake

STEM Challenge

Look at the picture and read the story.

STEM

Today is Caleb's birthday. He is having a party at the park. But to get to the park, his friends have to cross Crocodile Lake. They can't go around the lake, because there are trees that are too thick to walk through. They can't swim in the lake, because it's too deep and filled with crocodiles. Help Caleb's friends get to his birthday party by building a bridge that they can walk across to get to the park.

Crocodile Lake

STEM Challenge

Objective

Design and construct a bridge that will hold a group of "friends."

Challenge

- Bridge must be at least 2 inches high and 8 inches long
- Bridge must hold a group of "friends" (2 or more small toys or action figures) without falling or tipping over

Suggested Materials

- straws
- paper
- tape
- paper clips
- 2 or more action figures or small toys
- glue
- string

STEM Process

1 Ask

- What is a lake?
- Why does a bridge need to be strong or sturdy?
- How strong does a bridge need to be to hold 2 or more friends?

2 Plan

1. Look at the materials you have.
2. In the Plan box on the next page, draw a picture of the bridge you will build.

3 Create

Use the materials to build the bridge you drew.

4 Test

1. Stand your bridge upright. Is it at least 2 inches high and 8 inches long?
2. Place your "friends" (at least 2 small toys) on the bridge. Does the bridge stay standing? Is it strong enough to hold the friends?
3. In the Test box on the next page, draw a picture to show one thing that happened during the test.

Bodies of Water

Crocodile Lake

Plan

Create: Use materials to build your project.

Test

Did it work? ☐ yes ☐ no

Looking for Rocks

Read the text below to explain that rocks are part of Earth's crust and can be found everywhere. Then read the science story to your child.

Earth has a **crust**. It is mostly covered by water, soil, and plants. But under that, Earth's crust is **rock**.

Rocks can be big or small, and rocks can be **rough** or **smooth**.

Rocks can be found outside in a garden or a bridge.

Rocks can be found inside a home, on the floors or the walls.

Talk with Your Child Have your child look at the pictures above and point to the rocks. Talk about if the rocks look rough or smooth. Discuss the way rocks are formed and moved from place to place (smaller rocks break away from mountains and boulders and are moved by water, wind, animals, or people). Lastly, ask your child to point out the things in your house that are made of rock.

Concept: Rocks are part of Earth's land.

Science

Rocks Are Everywhere

Yesterday, Aunt Amy and I saw rocks everywhere! She said that rocks come from Earth's crust. Pieces of rock break away and end up in all sorts of places. We found rocks along the lake. When I got home, I found rocks in the garden and in the wall. Then I went inside and saw rocks in our kitchen! The countertop is made from a big piece of speckled rock. The floor is made from a smooth gray rock. Rocks are everywhere!

Looking for Rocks

Skills: Visual discrimination; Inference

Answer the question.

Color ☺ for **yes**. Color  for **no**.

1

Do rocks come in different sizes?

 yes  no

2

Do rocks break and make more rocks?

 yes  no

3

Can you find rocks in a garden?

 yes  no

4

Can your house have things that are made from rocks?

 yes  no

Looking for Rocks

Skills: Comparing; Categorizing; Visual discrimination; Inference

Look at the first picture. Then draw an **X** on the picture that does not belong.

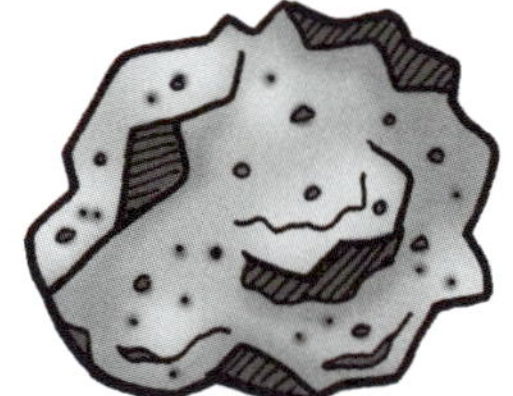

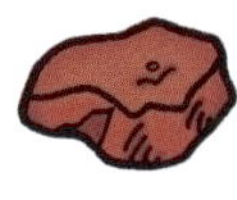

Looking for Rocks

Skills: Following directions; Visual discrimination; Colors

Color the smooth, round rocks brown.

Color the bridge made of rocks yellow.

Color the biggest rock gray.

Color the sharp rocks orange.

Looking for Rocks

Rock Tower

STEM Challenge

Look at the picture and read the story.

STEM

Lily the lizard needs to move to a new rock home. Lily looks around for the perfect home. She sees a tall rock tower she'd like to live in. Lily crawls to the rock tower, but Manny the lizard is already on top of it. Manny says to her, "Sorry Lily, this is my rock tower. Maybe you can build one of your own." Help Lily make a rock tower that is just as tall as Manny's.

Rock Tower

STEM Challenge

Objective

Design and construct a tower of rocks.

Challenge

- Tower must be as high as your knees
- Tower must stay standing for 30 seconds

Suggested Materials

- rocks of different sizes and shapes

STEM Process

1 Ask

- Where do rocks come from?
- What shapes and sizes are your rocks?
- Are your rocks smooth or rough?
- What would happen if you put a big rock on a small rock?
- What will help your tower to stay standing?

2 Plan

1. Look at the materials you have.
2. In the Plan box on the next page, draw a picture of the tower you will build with the materials.

3 Create

Use the materials to build the tower you drew.

4 Test

1. When you have finished building your tower, stand next to it. Does the tower reach your knees?
2. Count to 30 seconds. Is your tower still standing?
3. In the Test box on the next page, draw a picture to show one thing that happened during the test.

Looking for Rocks

Rock Tower

Plan

Create: Use materials to build your project.

Test

Did it work? ☐ yes ☐ no

Smart Start STEM

Certificate

____

Name

Congratulations!

You planned, created, and tested the things you made!

You solved problems and helped people!

Answer Key

Samples of completed STEM challenges are pictured below. These are meant to serve as examples of possible outcomes of the challenges. The outcome of each challenge will vary depending on the child's approach and the materials used.

Shapes, Sizes, and More

Page 10

Page 11

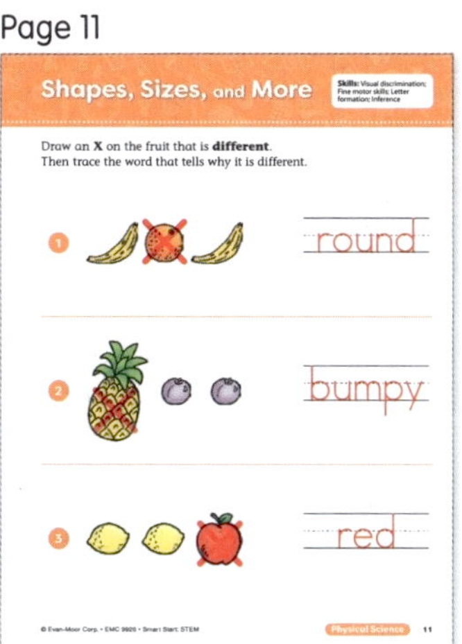

Page 12

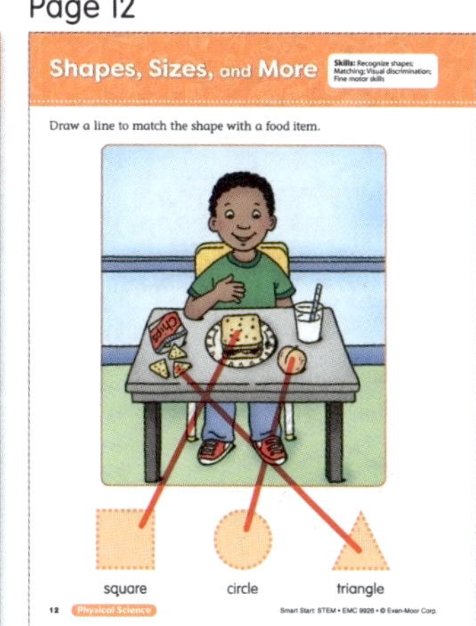

Sample of a completed **Fruit Basket** STEM Challenge

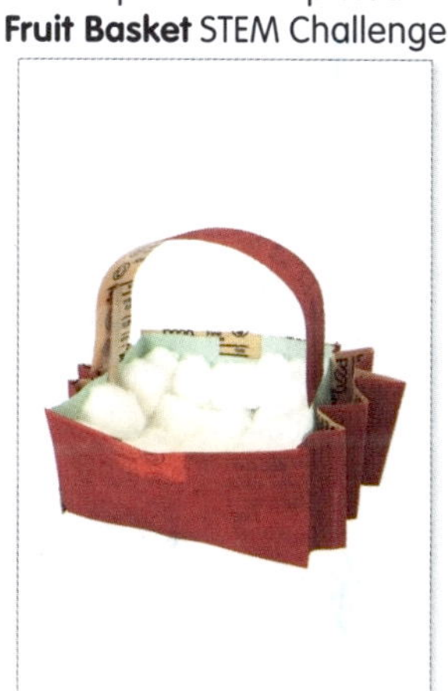

Solids and Liquids

Page 18

Page 19

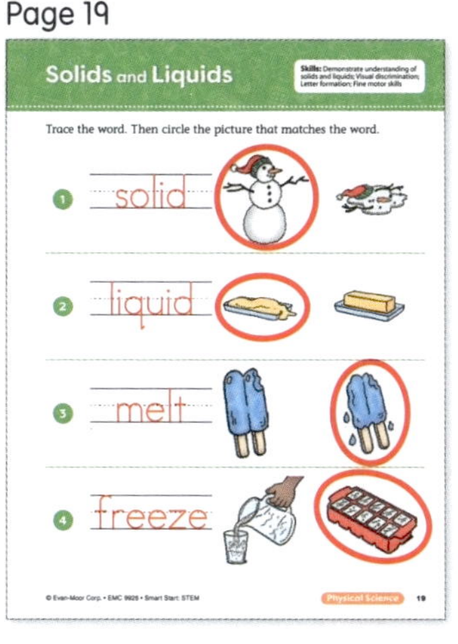

Page 20

Sample of a completed **Stay Cool** STEM Challenge

Does the Magnet Stick?

Page 26

Does the Magnet Stick?

Look at the picture. Will the object stick to a magnet?
Color yes if the object will stick to a magnet.
Color no if the object will not stick to a magnet.

YES NO

1 yes no 2 yes no
3 yes no 4 yes no

26 Physical Science Smart Start: STEM • EMC 9926 • © Evan-Moor Corp.

Page 27

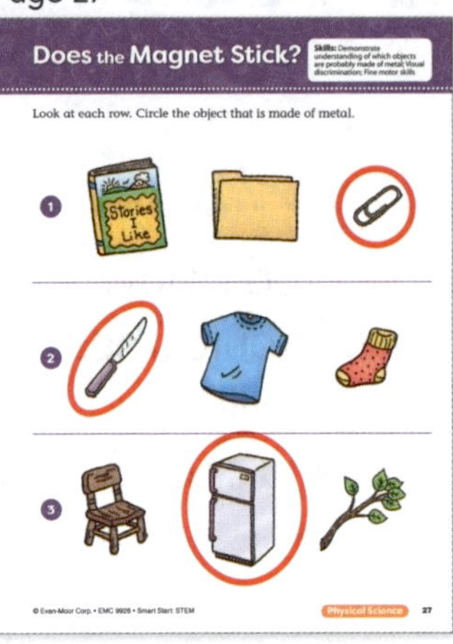
Does the Magnet Stick?

Look at each row. Circle the object that is made of metal.

1
2
3

© Evan-Moor Corp. • EMC 9926 • Smart Start: STEM Physical Science 27

Page 28

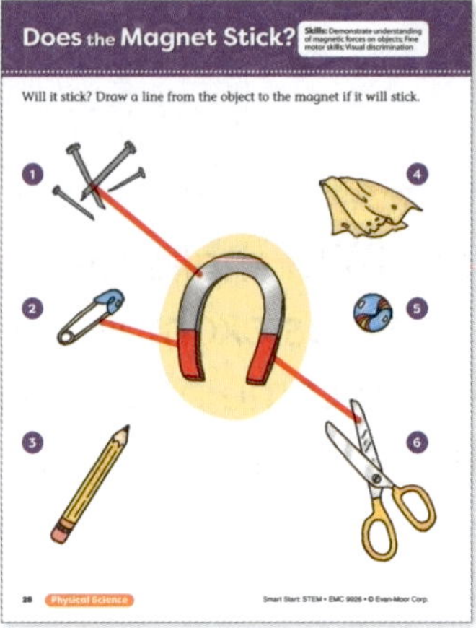
Does the Magnet Stick?

Will it stick? Draw a line from the object to the magnet if it will stick.

1 2 3 4 5 6

28 Physical Science Smart Start: STEM • EMC 9926 • © Evan-Moor Corp.

Sample of a completed
Magnet Painting
STEM Challenge

Wheels Do the Work

Page 34

Wheels Do the Work

Are the people using wheels to make work easier?
Color for **yes**. Color for **no**.

1 yes no 2 yes no
3 yes no 4 yes no

34 Physical Science Smart Start: STEM • EMC 9926 • © Evan-Moor Corp.

Page 35

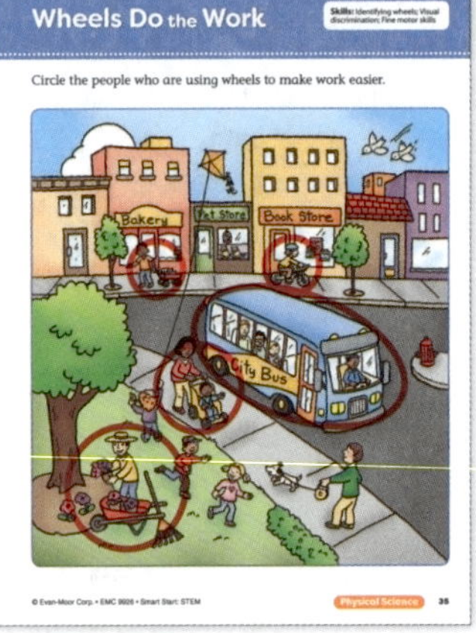
Wheels Do the Work

Circle the people who are using wheels to make work easier.

© Evan-Moor Corp. • EMC 9926 • Smart Start: STEM Physical Science 35

Page 36

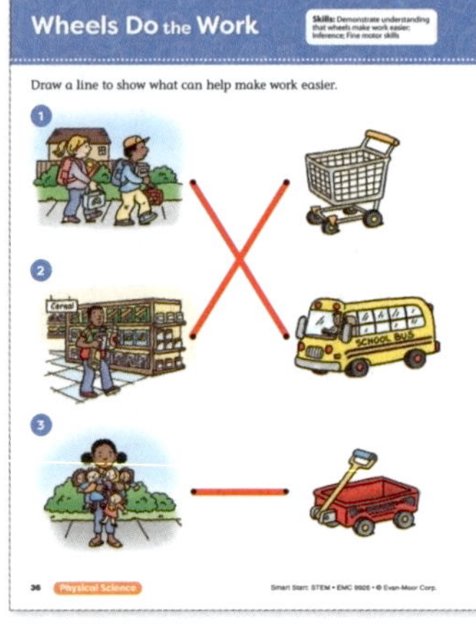
Wheels Do the Work

Draw a line to show what can help make work easier.

1 2 3

36 Physical Science Smart Start: STEM • EMC 9926 • © Evan-Moor Corp.

Sample of a completed
Gumdrop Wheel
STEM Challenge

What Plants Need

Page 42

What Plants Need

Answer the question.
Color for **yes**. Color for **no**.

1 Did this plant get water? yes no
2 Did this plant get water? yes no
3 Did this plant get sunlight? yes no
4 Did this plant have soil? yes no

42 Life Science Smart Start: STEM • EMC 9926 • © Evan-Moor Corp.

Page 43

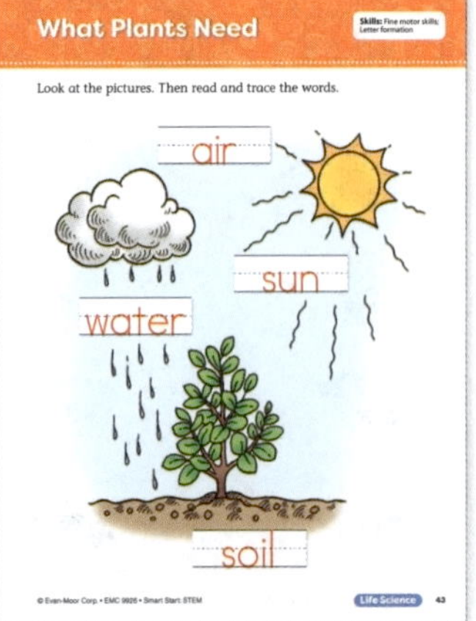
What Plants Need

Look at the pictures. Then read and trace the words.

© Evan-Moor Corp. • EMC 9926 • Smart Start: STEM Life Science 43

Page 44

What Plants Need

Draw what is missing to show what plants need.
Then draw flowers and color the picture.

44 Life Science Smart Start: STEM • EMC 9926 • © Evan-Moor Corp.

Sample of a completed
Thirsty Plants
STEM Challenge

What Animals Need

Page 50

What Animals Need

Answer the question.
Color ☺ for **yes**. Color ☹ for **no**.

1. Does a rabbit need food? yes no
2. Does a rabbit need shelter? yes no
3. Is this a safe place for a rabbit to live? yes no
4. Does a rabbit need fresh air? yes no

50 Life Science Smart Start: STEM • EMC 9926 • © Evan-Moor Corp.

Page 51

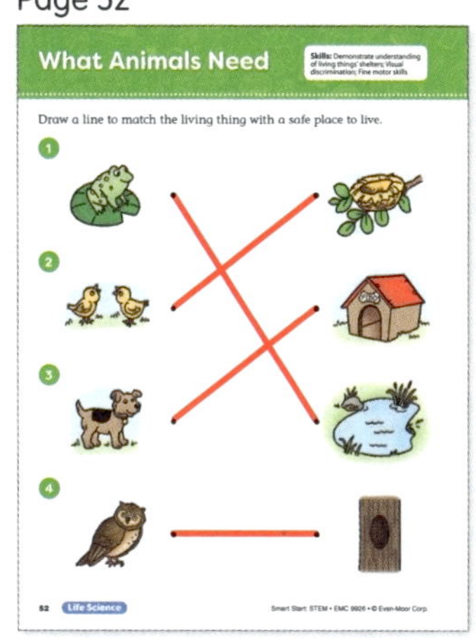
What Animals Need

Trace the words. Then color the pictures.

air

shelter

food

water

© Evan-Moor Corp. • EMC 9926 • Smart Start: STEM Life Science 51

Page 52

What Animals Need

Draw a line to match the living thing with a safe place to live.

1

2

3

4

52 Life Science Smart Start: STEM • EMC 9926 • © Evan-Moor Corp.

Sample of a completed
Bunny Cage
STEM Challenge

I'm Growing!

Page 58

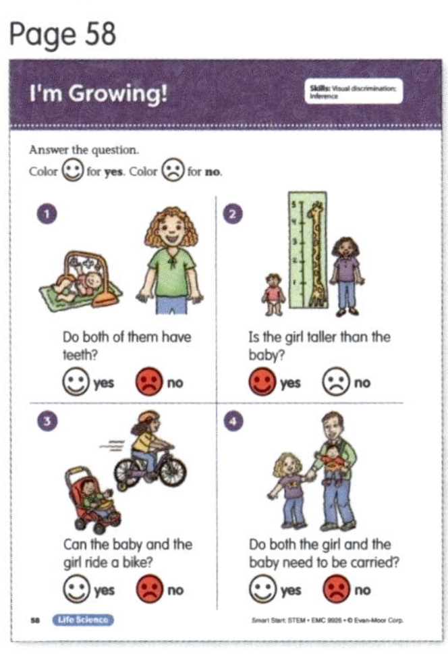
I'm Growing!

Answer the question.
Color ☺ for **yes**. Color ☹ for **no**.

1. Do both of them have teeth? yes no
2. Is the girl taller than the baby? yes no
3. Can the baby and the girl ride a bike? yes no
4. Do both the girl and the baby need to be carried? yes no

58 Life Science Smart Start: STEM • EMC 9926 • © Evan-Moor Corp.

Page 59

I'm Growing!

Draw a line to match then and now.

Then Now

1

2

3

4

© Evan-Moor Corp. • EMC 9926 • Smart Start: STEM Life Science 59

Page 60

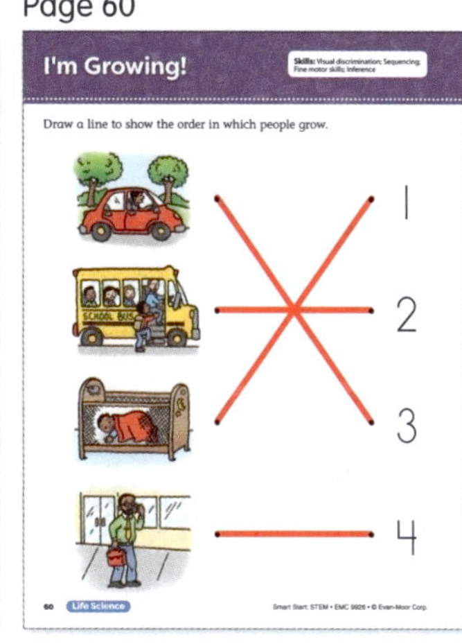
I'm Growing!

Draw a line to show the order in which people grow.

1

2

3

4

60 Life Science Smart Start: STEM • EMC 9926 • © Evan-Moor Corp.

Sample of a completed
Big Kid Bed STEM Challenge

Trees Have Parts

Page 66

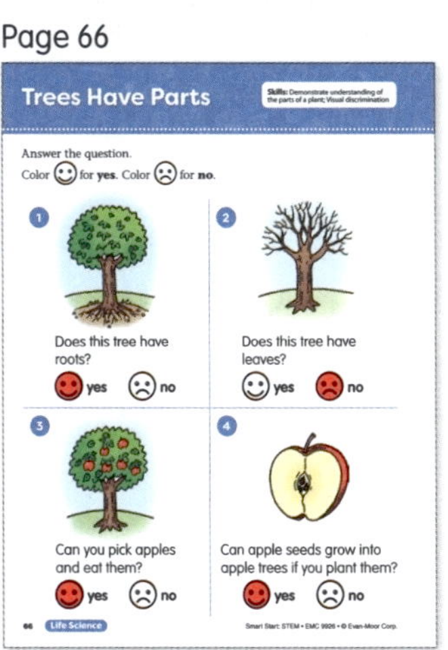
Trees Have Parts

Answer the question.
Color ☺ for **yes**. Color ☹ for **no**.

1. Does this tree have roots? yes no
2. Does this tree have leaves? yes no
3. Can you pick apples and eat them? yes no
4. Can apple seeds grow into apple trees if you plant them? yes no

66 Life Science Smart Start: STEM • EMC 9926 • © Evan-Moor Corp.

Page 67

Trees Have Parts

Trace. Then draw a line to the correct part in the pictures.

1. roots
2. trunk
3. leaves
4. seed

© Evan-Moor Corp. • EMC 9926 • Smart Start: STEM Life Science 67

Page 68

Trees Have Parts

Look at the first picture. Then circle the picture that does not belong.

1

2

3

4

68 Life Science Smart Start: STEM • EMC 9926 • © Evan-Moor Corp.

Sample of a completed
Tall Apple Tree
STEM Challenge

Animals Have Parts

Page 74

Page 75

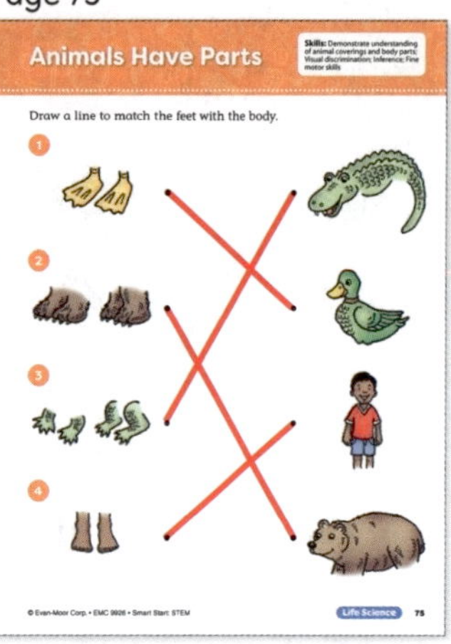

Page 76

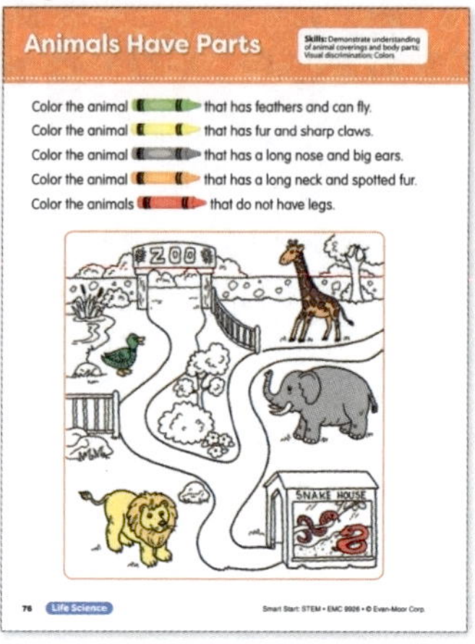

Sample of a completed **Animal Footprints** STEM Challenge

From Egg to Frog

Page 82

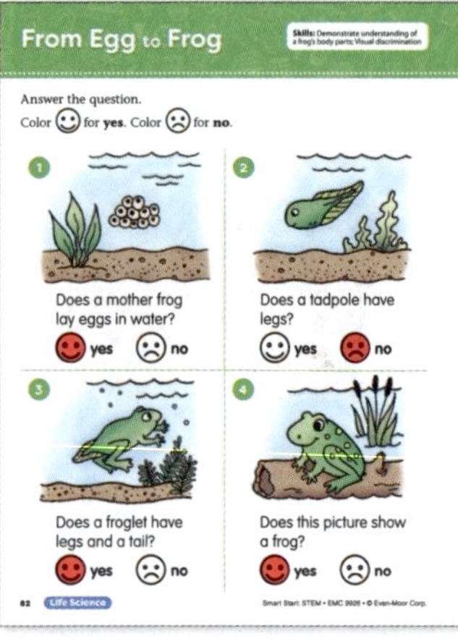

Page 83

Page 84

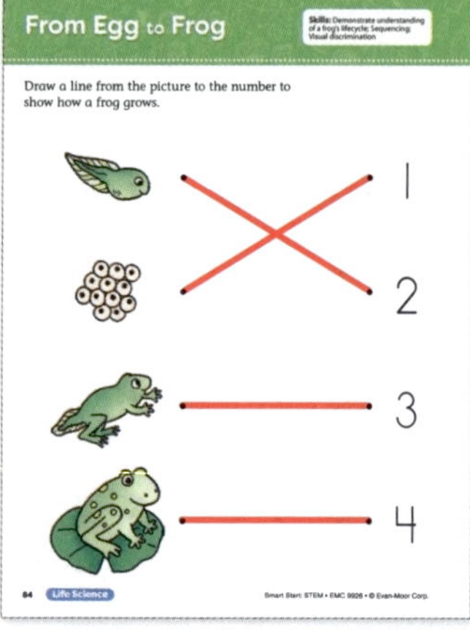

Sample of a completed **Lily Pad** STEM Challenge

Dinosaurs

Page 90

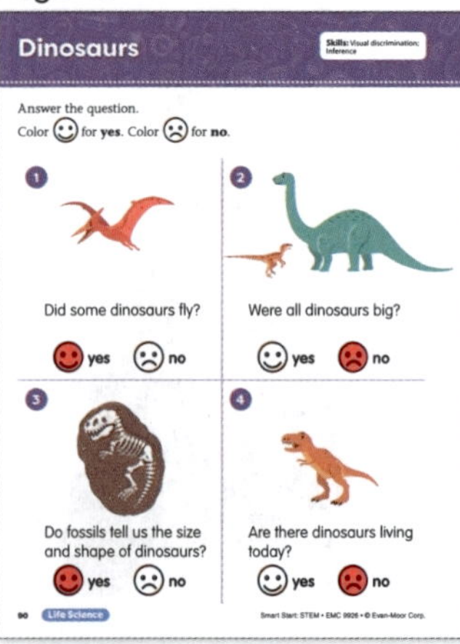

Page 91

Page 92

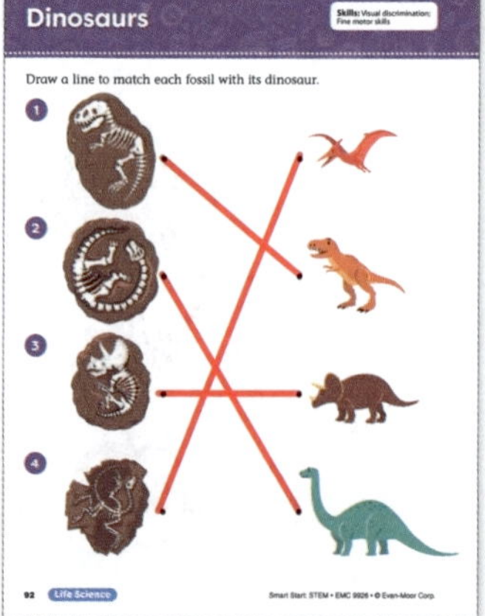

Sample of a completed **Dino Fossils** STEM Challenge

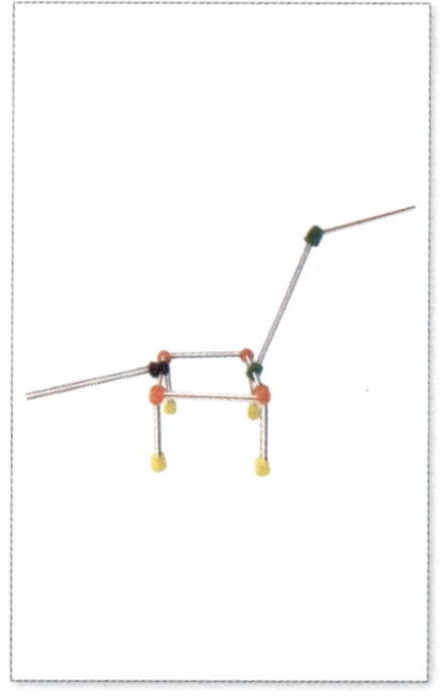

Four Seasons

Page 98

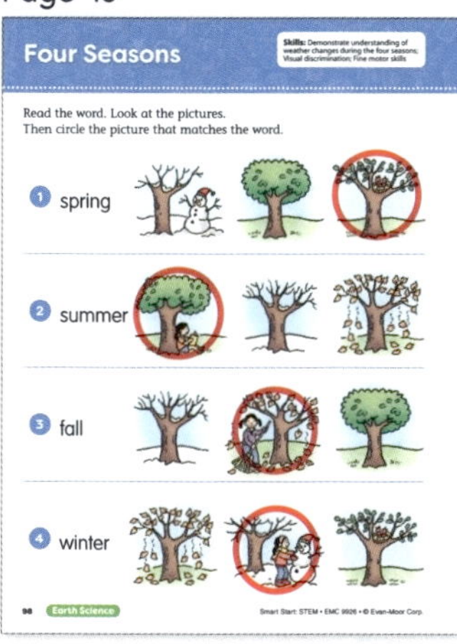

Page 99

Page 100

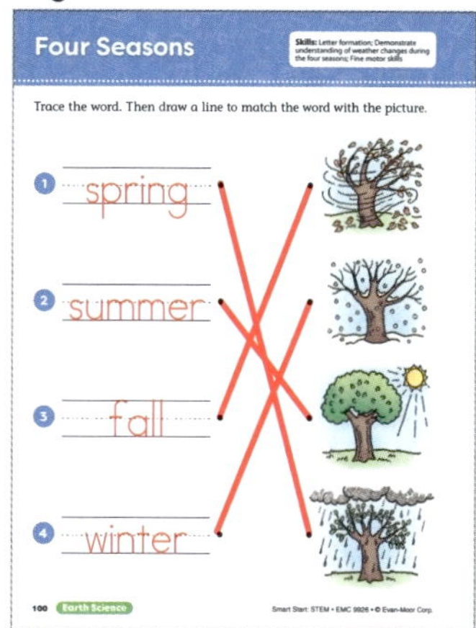

Sample of a completed **Leaky Roof** STEM Challenge

Bodies of Water

Page 106

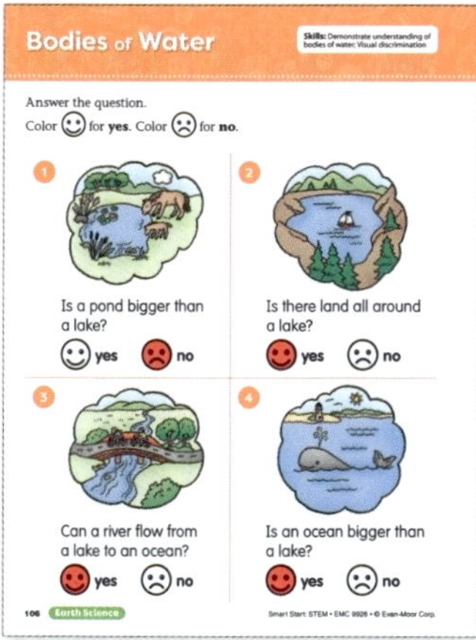

Page 107

Page 108

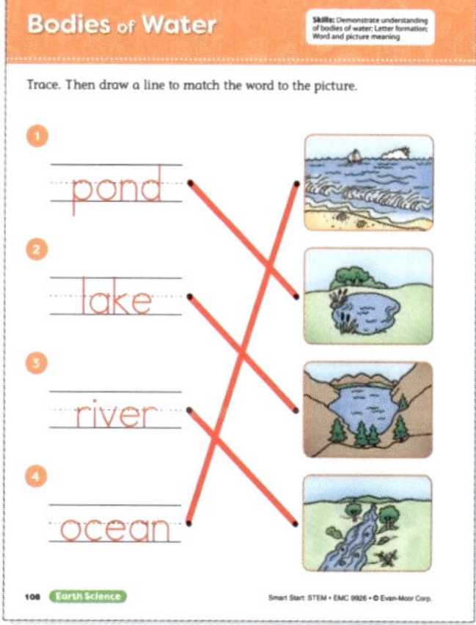

Sample of a completed **Crocodile Lake** STEM Challenge

Looking for Rocks

Page 114

Page 115

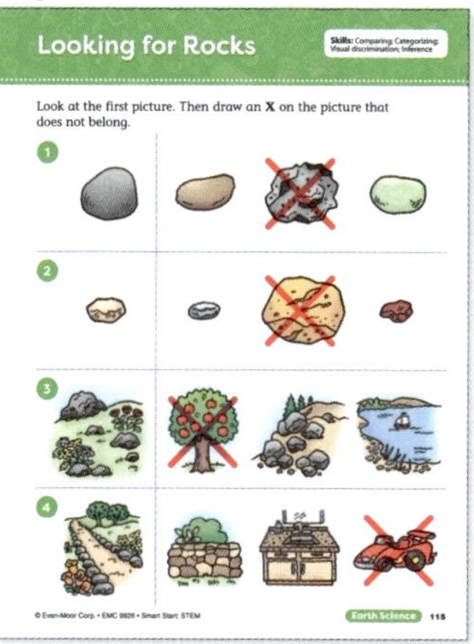

Page 116

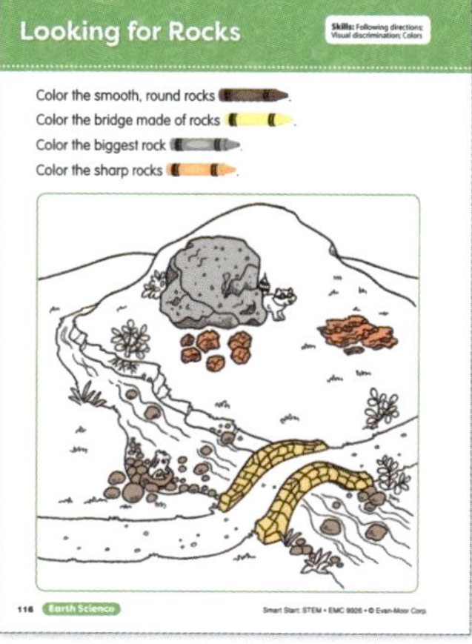

Sample of a completed **Rock Tower** STEM Challenge

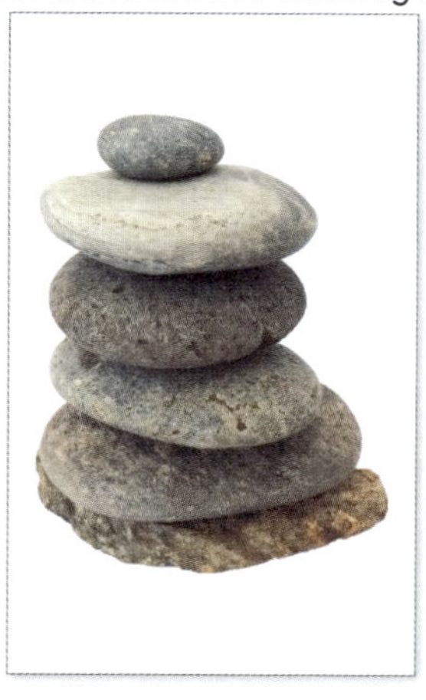